T0157304

Mr. Chandler's Wife

Stephanie M. Captain

authorHOUSE®

AuthorHouse™
1663 Liberty Drive
Bloomington, IN 47403
www.authorhouse.com
Phone: 1-800-839-8640

Published by AuthorHouse 6/11/2013

ISBN: 978-1-4817-3818-7 (sc)
ISBN: 978-1-4817-3819-4 (e)

Also by *Stephanie M. Captain*

Tobias Lincoln Hunt

A Hundred Things to Think About

East Wind

Dear God, We Need To Talk

Jehovah Answers

Cousin S.E. May

Our Time

Help Lord I Married A Golfer

Ulm Street

Sleep Walking in Church

Forever Family

P.A.S.T. Parenting as A Single Teenager

(Co-Authored with Ashley D. Captain)

Dedication

Not the man upstairs, but the one in my heart who loves me no matter what…Father God. Thank you for giving me your approval and your anointing.

Acknowledgements

The people who love me and stick with me through thick and thin-

My husband

My children---Amos II & Chantal, Ashley, & Aaron

My mother Beulah

My pastors Pamela & Winston Gardner

My sisters, brothers, god-parents and my friends

My Shekinah family

Simien and Asher---YaYa loves her babies

Special Thanks

My husband Amos who always pushes me to keep going when I am ready to give up. I love you honey. Thanks for giving me your ear, your arms, your shoulder, but most of all your heart.

Pastor Pamela Gardner for your support and encouraging words.

Shirlene Eaddy the friend that sticks closer than a brother—you have never stopped believing in me.

My daughter Ashley for helping me with each book I have written no matter how you felt or how busy her schedule.

TABLE OF CONTENTS

Chapter 1

At the far end of the house, the only source of light in the room was the computer monitor. With the exception of the humming of the modem the room was silent. Reclined in the plush leather chair he sat waiting, hoping, that eventually his expectation would be fulfilled. His desperation was for one thing and only she could give it to him. Everything about her was intoxicating; her smile, her touch, and her love. No matter how he'd tried to forget her or look the other way, he still fell prey to her alluring touch and her piercing eyes every time. Or was it that she was his victim?

It had been a month since the last time. Thirty long days and he had grown restless, irritable, and lonely. Everything in him cried out for her voice, her kisses, and the body he'd grown to need. Where was she? What was she doing? Was she happy? Did she miss him as much as he missed her? Why hadn't she contacted him? Thought after thought seize his heart until he grew weary of waiting and did what he'd promised himself he wouldn't do.

When the instant message chimed on the computer her heart instantly beat faster.

"I need to see you." He wasted no time getting right to the point.

"Hi and I miss you too…"

"I'm sorry, it's been so long and I just need to see you." His heart rate has risen with excitement.

"Ditto."

"Say it."

"Say what?"

1

"You know what I need to hear."

"What, that I miss you, can't wait to see you and touch you and love on you."

"Ah, music to my ears." He smiles in the dimly lit room.

She asks, "How's your day?"

"Better now. I don't like not being able to see you when I want to."

She strokes his ego, "Don't worry, I will make up for lost time, promise."

"So will I…promise." They both know he means what he says.

"I love it when you make me promises. Keeping your word brings me such ecstasy." He is unable to see her, but she is dancing around the room.

"Same place?"

"Yes, same place. I don't want to wait. This is so hard." Her body yearns for what only he can give her.

"I know. I wish it could be sooner but for now this is the way it has to be." He wants to satisfy her every wish and grows frustrated knowing she has to wait.

"I need you." She puts pressure on him knowing he will do anything to please her.

"We need each other."

"Room 259."

"I will be there." Letting out a sigh of relief he could finally get back to the pile of work on his desk. He'd been with her, if only for a little while, but it was enough to help him focus again. He didn't know when it had happened, but somewhere along the line she had before his addiction, and he had to have her no matter what others thought about it.

She returned to her family smiling, happy, and counting the days until.

There was no record, no witness; just the secret they shared. The guilt was there. The fear of being discovered was there, but the burning desire was greater than all of them.

When the computer chimed again his heart skipped a beat when her face popped up on the screen of his personal computer. Anxiously he accepted the request from her wanting to video chat live. There she was, beautiful, sexy, and his. The kind of woman men would kill for, and she was all his.

Chapter 2

The morning was passing very slowly. Hannah sat at her desk starring out of the large picture window. Her building was referred to as the guardian. It was located at the edge of the city and positioned to view its borders. High enough to view much of its activity from the many offices within it looked over the city from the north, south, east, and west. Most days she forgot there was a view, having so much work to complete. Lunch was something of a joke on her floor. There were many days she ate on the run while driving from one appointment to another meeting contractors and engineers. She worked from the time she placed her purse in the file cabinet until she heard the footsteps of others walking to the elevators. There was no time for personal phone calls or social visits, just work work work.

Hannah just wasn't feeling much like working. That particular morning it had been hard dropping her little baby off at her music class. She missed her immensely each time she had to leave her, but especially on Wednesdays. All she wanted to do was go home and bake cookies or something. Cuddle up and read her a story and watch her play. She was growing so fast and she knew lost moments would never be recovered. Obviously, no one had forced her to go the work, it was her choice. After having done anything except work how do you stop? How do you grant yourself permission for such a luxury? If she had known the answer to those questions, no doubt she would be at the park with her daughter.

The wind tenderly rustled the trees. Swaying back and forth in a slow dance to nature's command they honor the elements in obedience. Large dark clouds moved slowly in no particular hurry to get anywhere it seemed.

Change was on the horizon but this time she sensed it may not be for the better. Looking down at the pile of plans deposited on her desk did not make her feel any better. It was going to be a long day she could tell.

From time to time she thought about her husband. Something just wasn't right with them. She didn't know what, but it was there. His touch was different, his time always spent, and his body too tired to respond to what she needed. Still the doting father, the great provider, and the professional man just not so much in need of a wife. She missed him and they slept in the same bed; only the world was between them. They went to church every Sunday. Their weekends were spent with family and other friends and were methodical at best. He constantly checked his phone, needed to finish last minute work, or changed the subject. Each time she tried to speak to him about it he played it down or changed the subject. He found something to do around the house or some reason to leave the house.

"Morning Mrs. Chandler," Cliff, one of the big wigs pokes his head through her door. "We have donuts today. Better come quick because you know it's every man for himself."

"Good Morning," she smiles at his dry humor. Her line of work was still very much a man's world in so many instances. Paid far less for the very same job she was demeaned because of her gender. God forbid a woman decided to be a mother, it was used against her liken to having the plague. Not to mention she was the only female employee for seven floors at that particular building. The jokes were endless. 'The higher you go the less estrogen you'll know. If you can't hold your own, then just go home.' She didn't allow them to agitate her. She had her own sayings. "Mindless and spineless" and a few other terms she was still asking Jesus to help her not say or think. At the end of the day she always had Brice to talk over her day with, until lately when all that had changed.

The donuts and her absentee husband where lost in the hustle and bustle of the eleventh floor. By 2 o'clock she'd attended three meetings, completed five reports, almost slapped a co-worker, and repented at least ten times for what she wanted to do to him. All while feeling sick as a dog. Her job did not afford her the luxury of being ill, not in her case anyway. The pain medication had not provided any relief, nor the tea and deep breathing. Nausea and vertigo plagued her for several days now, but she could always get past it; not today. As long as she had energy she put it to good use. It was the sudden bouts of weakness that slammed into her like an eighteen wheeler that made her wonder and worry a bit.

When Bob comes in and finds her slumped over her desk the blood drained from his face. He was not like the others. He was a kind and gentle man who absolutely without a doubt loved God. He always had a good word or he said nothing at all; just being around him made her day go a whole lot smoother.

"Ms. Hannah I think you'd better gone on home now. No sense compromising your health. This job will be here when we're gone on God says the same. You go on home to that pretty little girl of yours and get yourself better you hear? I'll take care of you Ms. Hannah, promise."

Had anyone else spoken those words Hannah would have smiled and continued to make the most of it, but Bob's word meant something. He never said anything he did not do and he never made a promise he did not keep. Everyone in the building knew it to be true, even the parking lot attendants. Having worked for The Lyndell Corporation thirty-two years, the only day of work he'd missed was to bury his wife. He never called in, he never came late or left early, and he never lied. That was Bobby Grayson of Singleton, Maryland, 5'10 one hundred and eighty pounds, pleasantly bald, and southern Baptist---heart of gold. His word was all the encouragement Hannah needed to take her sick body home.

"Do you need me to drive you home? No problem at all Ms. Hannah. No problem at all?"

"Thanks Bob, but I'll be fine." Seeing the concerned look on his face she wanted to reassure him. Something in her heart told her he knew more about what was to come than she did.

"Then I'll ride with you down the elevator."

She knew not to try and stop him. Not when he takes her bag, or when he accompanied her to the car in the parking garage. As he stands on the curve waving as she drives away she knows without a doubt there is a God because she saw Him in Bobby Grayson every day.

Bob had been just the confirmation she had been waiting for to go home and get better. Driving home from work Mrs. Brice Chandler could not shake the uneasiness she felt that extended beyond the war going on within her body. After taking pain medication for her head and saying several silent prayers the pain and trepidation grew worse until she'd had no other choice but to brace herself for what she knew was coming. Called or sent her gut told her that life was about to become unbearable again. There were no tears, no anger, just hope that her family would make it. She'd heard it said often enough by people in her life that your faith had to be tested and she knew she was about to have an examination. The unnerving part was she did not know what material she would be required to know.

The last few weeks being the exception, her life was great. Much of the sorrow she carried all of her life was no more. For the most part she got along well with Brice's family. His mother was still a work in progress but she trusted God for where they had come. Her dream of having a big brother who loved her and looked out for her was the reality she lived. He loved his Hannah Banana and she loved her "T". For almost two years things had been so good it was almost scary. Sure she had some bumps in the road, but they were minor and having Jane and Johanna on her support team made things even the better. Why were things changing? There was no doubt in her mind that they were about to change.

Thinking better of picking up the baby early from her one day a week at daycare she steered the latest model, black crossover, a gift from her husband for their first anniversary, in the opposite direction. Wednesdays was her Mother's women's group and although Johanna had insisted on caring for her granddaughter on that day as well, she wanted her to enjoy her friends and have a free hand while doing it.

She longed to talk to Brice, but he had not been answering his phone. Funny how he went from checking on her several times during the day, surprising her with flowers for no reason at all, and bringing her little gifts, to having to be tracked down for a conversation with his wife. Some days it sadden her beyond belief, but she kept going because that was the only thing she knew to do. She could not talk to anyone about it. Who could you tell your most intimate secrets to but God anyway? Brice Chandler was just what she had been looking for all that time when she was afraid to love and be happy. He was what she needed, but she was certain interference was running somewhere in her marriage. She just did not know what to do about it and it was making her sick, literally.

Just before heading home Hannah decides to go ahead and fill her car with gasoline. She'd had to make some extra stops that week and was running a little low. Brice always took care of her vehicle, but that day she decided to take that off his hands. When she pulled into the service station she instantly became dismayed when the card she used was declined. She knew that was impossible. One reason being she almost never used the card. The other was that she knew her husband always put funds on the card each payday for her just in case needs. She was feeling worse and worse, but the situation annoyed her so much she could not let it go. Their bank was about a fifteen minute drive and her heart told her that was a drive she needed to take.

Her mind was on overdrive during those fifteen minutes. Playing out several scenarios in her head, the pain increased more and more due to the added stress. By the time it was her turn to be assisted she was already in defense mode.

"Next please." The teller's cheery voice worked on the jumbled, flaccid, seared nerves bombarding through Hannah's body.

"Yes. I'd like some account information please." Giving the required information the teller pulls up the account in question.

"How may I help you Mrs. Chandler?" The teller questioned in the same cheerful manner.

"I'm unable to use my bank card and I need to see if there has been some mistake." Her answer shocks Hannah.

"No Mrs. Chandler there is no mistake, your account is extremely low."

Smiling she slides the account information to the customer not expecting anything further. How grossly wrong was her assumption. Hannah's retort, "Excuse me. What do you mean by low Miss?" is offensive to the young lady.

"Meaning this is what you have in your account." Pushing a small yellow sticky note in front of her the teller continues to smile. When Hannah looks at the note with $1.63 cents, she almost curses and becomes quite arrogant.

"Ah, I know that's not right. We keep nothing less than $5,000 in this account so I need you to check again. Perhaps you keyed a number in incorrectly."

"Let me try again Mrs. Chandler, one moment please." After peeking on her keyboard long enough to have typed a business report, the teller shakes her head and replies, "The information you were given is correct Mrs. Chandler."

Feeling flushed, foolish, and fickle Hannah decides to enquire further. "How may I obtain a report on this account?"

"There will be a $5.00 charge for that service Mrs. Chandler, but I will be more than happy to assist you."

"No. I'm not paying you to tell me what is going on with my account when I allow you to invest my money. I want a courtesy report please."

"Ma'am I don't make the policies." The teller struggles with the smile and the blue eyes aren't so friendly anymore.

"How trite of me to think you could. Please allow me to speak to your manager."

The manager in question happened to be assisting a teller with a client two windows down and has overheard the conversation. One step ahead of defusing the situation she is already en route to provide the teller some back up. "How may I assist you Ma'am?" The blonde haired woman further annoys Hannah.

"I need to find out why my account, an account that I never use is extremely low. I understand that your bank charges a $5.00 fee for such a report. I also realize that you value your customers and should be more than willing to provide such a service as a courtesy. Especially since I have several accounts with your fine establishment."

The manager, who couldn't be much older than Hannah smiles and says, "Mrs. Chandler if you would follow me to my office I'll be happy to assist you." Walking to the office, that is no more than a few feet away, Hannah quickly tries to process the current situation.

"Have a seat Mrs. Chandler."

"Thank you." By now all courtesy is forced by both parties.

Curtly she demands, "May I see your identification again please? I will also need your account number."

By now Hannah is done with small talk and wants to get a little rude. She hears Jane in her head saying, "You have to be nasty sometimes because that is the only language some people understand." She does not know if the woman was only doing her job. Passing the requested information Hannah enjoys being off her feet for the moment. She knows her own personal pain or problems were no excuse for making others miserable so she decided to breathe and smile assuming that was what a good Christian was supposed to do.

"Do you believe your account has been compromised Mrs. Chandler? If so, we need to cancel this card immediately, and file a police report."

"I just know I haven't used the card in a year and there should be funds available. The report will allow me to see and make a determination as to what actions, if any, I should take based on my findings."

"Understood. Excuse me for a minute while I retrieve that information from the printer." In less than a minute the manager as promised returns, report in hand. "Here is the information you requested Mrs. Chandler. Should you require any further assistance please feel free to come back and see me. Here's my card."

"Thank you very much Ms. Brown."

"My pleasure, have a great day Mrs. Chandler."

Hannah replies, "You as well" and exits the office. Walking to the car Hannah had no doubt her sudden change of attitude had everything to do with her realization that Mrs. Corel-Waiters Chandler had another account with funds exceeding half a million dollars in it at the very same bank. People were so phony. She guessed the Bible was right when it said that "money answered all things."

It took time to recover from the long painful walk to and from the bank's parking lot. She was annoyed by the fact that she had to even come because someone had been foolish enough to make what she was sure was a mistake with her money. Feeling bleak and dismal, she knew she needed the rest. Leaning back in her cream leather chair she closed her eyes and asked God for some help for whatever was coming. Finally getting to the information she becomes puzzled when seeing purchases that just did not make sense. Odd things like furniture, jewelry, hotels, and boutique purchases were consistent for the entire length of the statement. It was ludicrous to her.

Deciding to go back to the same Ms. Brown to enquire a bit further she opens the car door to make her way to the lobby once more, but instantly realized her body would not allow such a task. She had to go home or she was sure someone would discover her lying in the parking lot. Slowly putting the car in reverse Hannah travels home; determined to get to the bottom of things the following day. She and Brice would decide just how to handle such a problem together. If it was one thing Brice Chandler did not play around with it was money. That made her feel a little more peace about the situation, he would know just what to do.

Chapter 3

The alarm system's alert that a door had opened to the residence went unnoticed. The room was consumed with them and them alone. Infiltrated with emotions, desire, and pure sexual lust they only had eyes for each other and were oblivious of the third pair of eyes that had entered the room. She was all he could think about and they both knew something must change to make their union a more permanent one.

At the far end of the house, the only source of light in the room was the computer monitor. With the exception of the humming of the modem the room was silent. Reclined in the plush leather chair he sat waiting, hoping, that eventually his expectation would be fulfilled. His desperation was for one thing and only she could give it to him. Everything about her was intoxicating; her smile, her touch, and her love. No matter how he'd tried to forget her or look the other way, he still fell prey to her alluring touch and her piercing eyes every time. Or was it that she was his victim?

It had been a month since the last time. Thirty long days and he had grown restless, irritable, and lonely. Everything in him cried out for her voice, her kisses, and the body he'd grown to need. Where was she? What was she doing? Was she happy? Did she miss him as much as he missed her? Why hadn't she contacted him? Thought after thought seize his heart until he grew weary of waiting and did what he'd promised himself he wouldn't do.

When the instant message chimed on the computer her heart instantly beat faster.

"I need to see you." He wasted no time getting right to the point.

"Hi and I miss you too…"

"I'm sorry, it's been so long and I just need to see you." His heart rate has risen with excitement.

"Ditto."

"Say it."

"Say what?"

"You know what I need to hear."

"What, that I miss you, can't wait to see you and touch you and love on you."

"Ah, music to my ears." He smiles in the dimly lit room.

She asks, "How's your day?"

"Better now. I don't like not being able to see you when I want to."

She strokes his ego. "Don't worry. I will make up for lost time, promise."

"So will I…promise." They both know he means what he says.

"I love it when you make me promises. Keeping your word brings me such ecstasy." He can't see but she is dancing around the room.

"Same place?"

"Yes, same place. I don't want to wait. This is so hard." Her body yearns for what only he can give her.

"I know. I wish it could be sooner but for now this is the way it has to be." He wants to satisfy her every wish and grows frustrated knowing she has to wait.

"I need you." She puts pressure on him knowing he will do anything to please her.

"We need each other."

"Room 259."

I will be there." Letting out a sigh of relief he could finally get back to the pile of work on his desk. He'd been with her, if only for a little while, but it was enough to help him focus again. He didn't know when it had happened, but somewhere along the line she had before his addiction, and he had to have her no matter what others thought about it.

She returned to her family smiling, happy, and counting the days until.

They thought there was no record, no witness; just the secret they shared. The guilt was there. The fear of being discovered was there, but the burning desire was greater than all of them.

When the computer chimed again moments later his heart skipped a beat when her face popped up on the screen of his personal computer. Anxiously, he accepted the request to video chat live. There she was, beautiful, sexy, and his. The kind of woman men would kill for and she was all his.

With a soft seductive tune playing in the background she began to slowly dance around the room playing peek-a-boo with certain parts of her body. Then she motioned for him to come closer with an enticing finger. Piece by piece she began to slowly undress before him. The black one piece designer evening gown shimmied to the floor leaving her in a black and red polka dotted bra and panty set. Knowing she almost had him ready to get in the car and find her she continued her show. For a few seconds she teased him with the clasp on her bra opening and closing it until, in a choreographed motion, it glided to the floor exposing her breast. Before removing her only remaining piece of clothing, she danced around the room for him; doing twists and turns, splits and bends that would make a priest sweat. Finally she sat on a nearby chase with both legs in the air and pulled the polka dotted underwear to her feet and tossed them across the room. Again she beckoned to him with her finger, turned around and walked naked to the king sized bed in the background. She sat; crossed her legs and once more called him to her. By then he was in a frenzy of lust and jumped up and said, "I'm coming baby! At work tomorrow, our place, I will be waiting."

Hannah is paralyzed in grief, rage, and betrayal until her lungs reminded her she must breathe. Feeling like someone had lunged into her a huge breath escapes from her and filled the room. That's when he realized they are not alone. Hannah felt sick to her stomach and sprinted down the hall in an attempt to find a place for the guile that she now felt for her husband. He doesn't know what she is going to do or what she is running to get. She was a good shot and if she was going for the gun he was a dead man. In an attempt to cut her off he ran through the Jack and Jill bathroom to get to the gun case before she did. Only she didn't head that way. She went pass that room and turned left into the half bath in the hall; vomiting profusely until she is positive her system is utterly empty, just like she felt. Splashing water on her face, she stood up and there he was in the mirror standing behind her. For a second their eyes locked in battle until in rage she demanded, "How could you Brice…how could you? I thought you loved me."

"I do love you Han, I do. I'm sorry Han, oh God, I'm so sorry."

He wasn't broken, just caught, and saying anything he needed to until he could come up with a plan and she knew it.

With venom she yelled, "How could you say that when you have a mistress? You love me so much you are sticking it to someone else Brice! That's how much you love me? You're lucky I don't blow your brains out and plead insanity. I'm sure I could get away with it."

"Don't say things you don't mean."

"You don't know what I mean. Apparently you don't know much about me do you? You thought I would never find out didn't you? You are a dog Brice and I find no use for you."

"Please Han, listen."

"Listen to what Brice? What possible reason could you have for such behavior?"

"Sometimes I just need more Han. I know there is no excuse, but I just…I don't know, I can't explain it."

"More of what! Sex, obedience, love; more of what? How is this my fault! Saying you need implies that I didn't do something or I wasn't good enough."

"Maybe we got married too soon."

"Well Brice, today is your lucky day because I can fix that in about thirty days."

"Thirty days?"

"That's all it takes for us to be divorced and you can be with her. You can be free of your wife, the one you stood before God and family and said you loved and would always be there for. The one you said you would be true to, remember that Brice Anthony Chandler. You lying, cheating, no good son of a…"

He cut her off. "See, that right there. She doesn't speak to me in that manner, even if she's upset with me."

"How dare you! How dare you compare me to that whore! I will beat you to a pulp! Do you hear me!" Their voices escalated to the point that the neighbors are now suddenly concerned for the perfect family that was always so quiet and friendly. Especially Ms. LuAnn; she was frantic with worry to the point that she started to rock back and forth like a child who is distraught.

"It sounds like she makes you happy. So go and do you Brice, just go." Her heart was crushed and breathing was labored.

"She does and I didn't mean for it to happen."

"So you love her?"

"I don't know Hannah, I like the way she makes me feel, like a man."

"I thought I made you happy, remember? You were the one that insisted on us being married. How could you love another woman when you have a wife? The wife you said was all you ever wanted."

"I didn't say I was in love with her."

"You didn't say no to the question Brice. If you did not love her you would have said no. That tells me everything. Help yourself Brice Anthony Chandler, help yourself. My daughter and I are out of here. I promise you I will never set foot in this house again. Go be with her since she makes you so happy. You've found your life after screwing up ours. Now Joy and I must find our own life. Connor treated me far better than this and he was better in bed too."

That hit him just where she wanted it to. Wanting to deliver another fatal blow to his ego she repeated, "Joy and I will have nothing further to do with you ever again."

"No Han please! Please don't leave me. Please don't take my little girl away from me." He looked distraught. The kind of broken that none of the kings' horsemen nor the kings' men could ever repair.

"You haven't touched me in weeks and now I know why. You prefer to play with the baby and anything else not to be in the same room with me. You are such a liar! I hate you Brice! Every time I asked you what was wrong you said nothing. Every time I asked if we were okay you said yes; when you and I both knew something wasn't right. You are a liar and a cheater and I wish you die the cruelest death possible! How could you lie to me! You were supposed to be different, but you are just a sad excuse for a husband and I hate the very sight of you. You are just another weak spineless man!! Get out of my way so I can get out of this hell hole."

By now she was screaming, crying, and throwing whatever she could get her hands on. Between ducks, he tried to talk, beg, anything, but she was in a place he had never seen her before. Her eyes were almost fixed and she was unwilling to hear one more thing from him.

"No Hannah. Please Hannah, I'm sorry, please forgive me! Don't leave me! Don't take my family away from me. I need my family. Don't take my little girl away."

When he put his hand out to stop her she looked at him with such an evil that it startled him. He stepped back and she pushed past him. Before slamming the door she turned around and said, "Maybe now you and the woman you love can start your own family!" The boom from the door closing rattled the entire living room. It caused some of Brice's weight lifting trophies to come crashing down to the hard wood floor, along with their wedding picture that hung over the fireplace. She didn't see Miss. LuAnn's mother, Ms. Penny pacing back and forth on the side of the yard as she drove off. Whenever something upset her thirty year old mentally retarded daughter it upset her. Not being able to come next door and play with little Joy and talk to Mrs. Hannah was definitely going to upset her daughter.

After driving around for hours, Hannah pulled up to a hotel; mentally exhausted and heart broken. Joy had finally fallen asleep. She'd cried for her daddy until fatigue and grief caused her to collapse. She wanted her bedtime story, her cuddle and kisses, and for daddy to tuck her into bed and lay there with her until she fell asleep. Her normal routine since she'd come into the world. Her sad little eyes were too much for her mother's already shattered heart and she just did not know how to console either of them. Ignoring her husband's calls she finally turned off the phone. Going to her mother's home was not an option. She would say forgive him and work it out. She would say how God could do anything and heal anything, but she wasn't sure if she wanted God to heal her marriage. Brice had become her everything. She had given him her all and still it had not been enough. Nothing could change that. What could erase the reminder that what brought her so much pleasure, satisfaction, and even made her a better person was now the sole source of all her pain? Did he ever love her? Had it ever been about her or just the baby? Her entire life had been about pleasing her husband and being the best wife and mother she could be but he still found someone else to take her place.

Jane was most definitely out of the question. She would probably be willing to help her plan his murder by cooking up a plate of death by Etouffee, execution by Gumbo or some other Cajun sauce. If that wasn't feasible she would have been more than willing to have one of her most distant relatives walk him out to a wooded area so she could collect the insurance policy. He wasn't worth murder. He wasn't worth losing her child for. Not the one in the back seat or the one she was carrying. She'd done it his way. Connor was a thing of the past because that was what Brice wanted even though somewhere in the back of her mind she wrestled often with the truth that he still deserved to know he was a father. Whether he chose to embrace it or shun it, he deserved to know. Learning the truth about Miss. Ann had solidified that for her. Yet, Brice said no so that had been the final answer on the subject. She thought about Tobias and Kelly but like most of their friends, to them Brice was the perfect person. Hannah was lucky to have him. Some luck.

Although heartbroken there was also another emotion plaguing her. Strangely enough, in the midst of her crisis she felt relief stirring within her. There was no greater husband than Brice Chandler she was sure of it. He had been her hero, her savior of sorts, and there was nothing that she or Joy could ever ask for. He was provider, husband, and all around saint. For that reason she'd spent their entire marriage trying to please him and show him how much she appreciated all he had done for their family. Cooking his favorites, keeping the house perfect, keeping Joy perfect because he had a problem with her not wearing, eating, and playing with the best. Her entire life was centered around and engrossed in him. They did what he wanted, when he wanted, and how he wanted and it was all her idea. Despite returning to work after Joy's first birthday she still managed to pop in on him at work wearing just the right thing. She planned just the right candlelight dinners, and still gave him enough sex to overdose any man. All while staying active with their daughter, the church, and maintaining her relationships with family; right to the point of exhaustion. She did everything to make him want to stay, but always carried around the fear that one day he would up and leave like everyone else. She told herself she didn't deserve him. How he was too good for her and his mother had been quick to amen that fact every chance she got, behind his back of course. So she worked and worked and worked and did it his way, just like with Connor. The kind of sex he wanted, the foods he ate, the way he chose to run their household, and it was all so much hard work. Brice never had to ask for anything. It was already done before he had a chance to need or want it.

Life was perfect it seemed until the past few weeks. She knew something was wrong. Her feelings never lied to her, if anything they had gotten stronger after she'd joined the women's Bible study group at their church. No matter how she prayed, that feeling wouldn't leave. No matter how she asked him what was wrong he denied any such thing. Finally one morning, after her prayer time with Johanna, who had very much become her mother in every way, she got the feeling that she would find out soon enough. She hadn't felt like that since the day she found out about Miss. Ann being her birth mother.

Her mind began to wonder back to that day; the day Miss. Ann showed up on her doorstep. That day she sat on the floor of the bathroom and cried and cried until she was hoarse, until all her tears dried up, until she didn't have the strength to pull herself up or out of the black hole she'd fallen into. She'd wrestled with God. She thought the truth was supposed to make her free. Why did she feel like she was choking to death then? She was aware of Brice and little Joy sitting on the other side of the door but could not open it. As much as she knew Brice hurt for her and their daughter, as much as he hurt by her shutting them completely out, she still needed that distance. Her baby cried for the breast milk she was dependent upon her to give her but she had disconnected. Her mother was a monster. Her mother was an evil witch and she hated her with every fiber of her being. She'd wanted to check out of this world but she knew she couldn't orphan her baby. Who would care for Joy? She was positive no one could love her like she would. Still she could not see how to live past the moment she was living in. Until out of the dark place her soul was living she felt these words spoken to her heart, "I'm with you Hannah, lean on Me." That gave her the strength to get up, flush the bottle of medication down the toilet, and unlock the door. It was hard to believe it had been almost two years since that day. Yet she still knew that God remained with her and she could lean on Him as much as she'd learn how up until this point in her life. She knew that most of her leaning had been on Brice of whom she had made her king and her mother Johanna whom she thought knew just as much about the Bible as God did.

Chapter 4

When the sun came up, Hannah Renee was sitting in the middle of the king size bed holding her baby. The beautiful red tresses cascaded around her perfect face. Her beige skin with just a hint of brown was still moist from her bouts of crying for her daddy all during the night. She still did not know what to tell her. How much could an almost two year old comprehend? She knew routine, structure, and familiarity, none of which she was being given at the time. The only thing Hannah knew was the old familiar pain that had returned with a vengeance. The only plan she had was feeding Joy when she awakened and checking out at eleven a.m. She did not grasp life beyond that. It was Friday, but she'd called out for the first time in the year that she had become a civil engineer at the Lyndell Corporation. Probably the most stressful, gender bias, economic shifting employment she'd ever had, but it served its purpose.

When the phone rang it hurt to ignore her mother whom she knew was only concerned for her, but she had no strength to speak to anyone. No, she didn't deserve it, but she would not break down in front of her baby and if she talked to Johanna Hemsley she was certain this would become the case. She wasn't sure if Brice had filled her in, but her thoughts on the matter were a definite no. He did not want the wrath of God on him. Johanna may be a woman of the cloth, but it was crystal clear that she was a mother first, and a very over protective one at that. She missed their morning prayer that had been a part of their life since Hannah first told her about being pregnant and married. On a normal morning she would have dropped off Joy to her, had a cup of tea, prayed and then headed north on loop 410 to the high rise where testosterone ruled; Wednesdays being the only exception. Instead she sat in a state of shock still wearing the cloths she'd worn to work the previous day holding the one person in life she knew she could never live without.

By the end of the day the only thing she'd managed was going to a local department store for personal items for the two of them and paying for another day in the hotel. Strangely, she did not consider the possibility of running into someone she knew. Her heart was broken and she just did not know what to do with it. Her mind replayed over and over the last few weeks in her head. Question after question waltzed through her mind until her Joy demanded her attention for some reason or another. All she wanted to know was why?

What did I do? Why didn't he tell me? Why wasn't I enough? What does she have that I don't? Was I too skinny? Too ugly? When did I stop satisfying him? And finally, how could he? The truth that he had been caught lead her to believe that it wasn't something he ever intended giving up. She knew he wasn't sorry for hurting her and that made it easy to ignore his calls and his text. He had been her first love, the one she gave her virginity to after holding on for so long. She ran from him to Connor, only to run right back into the arms she had not wanted to leave in the first place. She gave him time and space to move on although he had begged her to stay with him. She felt that since he'd waited that long it must have been meant to be. Now she concluded that it was the baby he wanted all along and that men were dogs who would hump anything with a uterus.

They passed the afternoon watching cartoons and playing twenty-one questions as to why daddy wasn't there. She felt bad about lying to Joy but what else could she do? When the phone lit up again for what felt like the one millionth annoying time it was none other than Ms. Lucy. She drove a white minivan that had Jesus written all over it, literally. The front said, "Got Jesus!" the back said, "Jesus, don't leave home without Him." The sides said, "The best high you'll ever have." You could hear her coming long before you ever saw her because the bangle bracelets she wore clanged together symphonically as she waved her hands back and forth in a fly swatting motion praising God for one more thing He had done for her. She was guaranteed to be packing. Somewhere in her tote bag was a King James Version of the Holy Bible, disinfecting wipes, hand sanitizer, a bag of soft peppermint candy, and yes a little pink twenty-two caliber pistol. Some days she decided to leave the make-up at home. It was only on special occasions she wore her beehive wig or chandelier church hats, but she always without a doubt had a smile just for you. That was as sure as her catching the spirit every Sunday at church, at weddings, funerals, and at family graduation ceremonies. Brown skinned, brown eyes, five feet something, soon to be told that the social security thing was a myth, and I got a man and his name is Jesus, you were surely never to forget her once you met her. It was something about her that drew people to her, made them desire to linger in her presence, and covet her hugs. Not to mention her lemon pound cake. Somehow she always knew when to call; this day was no different.

"Hello Sister Chandler I don't know what's going on but all I do know is that I had a dream you was fighting and you was fighting. At first it was little snakes then they got bigger and bigger. Then one minute you would be trying to kill a snake and strangest thing is it would turn into a person then back to a snake and you was so confused. Then you turned around and the biggest snake of all was dragging your baby off into a cave. I guess your poor heart just couldn't take it no more cause you fainted. That's when I woke up screaming Jesus and throwing holy oil everywhere! Oh Sister I think I ruint my carpet. But it don't matter cause I done prayed till I know whatever the devil trying to throw your way is gonna go right back and knock him upside the head instead. You hear me! He gonna lose this one Sister Chandler; he won't win!"

Hannah felt like she was in some sort of dream and couldn't wake up. The dream where you want to scream but you have no voice. The one where someone is chasing you and you keep running and running, but it is dark and you can't see and then the inevitable happens, you fall down and no matter how you try, you can't get up. So there you lay in the pitch black of the night, injured, with footsteps approaching and there is nothing you can do except wait.

"Sister Chandler, you there?"

"Yes Ms. Lucy, I'm here." She didn't think she could ever get used to calling anyone sister or brother, so she did the respectful thing.

"Oh don't you worry none now Sister Chandler. Me and Mother Jo got this baby. We gonna keep praying and praying until you shoutin the victory."

"Thank you so much Ms. Lucy. I really appreciate you taking the time to call and to pray for me."

"Oh that's what I'm posed to do. We have to look out for each other."

"Well I really appreciate it."

"You know, you don't have to pretend with me. I feel your pain. I know you're hurting and I wish I could tell you it will be ok, but the truth is, sometimes it gets worse before it gets better. Oh but it will get better. You just remember that. It will get better."

For a few moments she is lost in her thoughts again until the crashing sound of the hotel lamp jars her back to the conversation.

"Ms. Lucy I have to go, little Joy just purchased a lamp for me."

"Uh oh." A chuckling Ms. Lucy says, then a quick, "Talk to you soon."

"Bye."

After cleaning up the mess, calling the front desk, feeding, bathing, and putting Joy to sleep, Hannah decided it was time to call her mother.

"Sweet Jesus baby, I don't know whether to be upset or relieved. I've been worried sick about you."

"I'm sorry Mommy…" Becoming a bit choked up she pauses and clears her throat. "I just had to get away. I didn't mean to hurt you or worry you I just felt like I was suffocating."

"What's going on Baby Girl? Brice just said you had a fight and you left and took the baby with you. He's worried about you baby."

"I have no interest in what is going on with Brice Mommy."

"That's your husband so I find that hard to believe. You loved him enough to marry him, so what's changed?"

"Mommy I really don't want to talk about it right now. I have some important decisions to make and…"

"Baby all married couples have spats. You are going to have some rough days and even tough weeks, but it is well worth going through it to get to the good stuff."

"It's over Mommy. I have no intention of going back. That is the only thing I am sure of right now."

"Oh dear." Johanna spoke it without realizing it. "Are you and my granddaughter well?"

"Yes Mommy we're fine. I mean as well as can be expected. Joy keeps crying for him Mommy and it breaks my heart, but I can't go back, and sadly enough I wish he would die a slow and torched untimely death."

"Hannah Renee! Oh Hannah may God not open His ears to your words."

"And may the devil carry out every letter."

"Then it's true. The dream Lucy Mae Fritters had about you. I didn't want to believe it but in my heart I knew. I just knew. You all have been so happy baby, what happened? What got you to this point?"

"He's cheating Mommy. He has someone else."

"How do you know this?"

"I came home early because I was ill and was surprised to see his car in the driveway. When I walked in the house I could hear voices but didn't know where they were coming from. Then I realized that Brice must be working from home so I decided to go and lie across the bed and let him work until I heard a woman's voice."

"You mean she was in your house?" a shocked and angry voice interjects.

"Yes. I mean no. He was talking to her. She was streaming on a video call. He was telling her how much he missed her and needed to see her again. Then she said, "Just watch my sweet teddy bear," and there she was undressing for him piece by piece as he drooled, moaned and groaned. Eventually she stood there naked describing erotically everything she was going to do to him and just how she would do it, all while touching her body as she spoke. At first I thought it was pornography but then I realized that not only was it his lover, but she had been for some time. Obviously they have been meeting at a hotel outside of town whenever they got the hots for each other and at work when they couldn't wait. When she finally finished stripping down to nothing but her fake fingernails she said, "See you at work tomorrow" and blew him a kiss. That's when I threw up."

"Where are you Baby Girl?"

"At a hotel not far from Joy's music class. We're doing okay Mommy, I promise."

"Where? I'm coming to get you right now so start packing."

Hannah could hear her mother set the alarm for the house and open the garage. Judging by the sound of her voice she knew not to argue.

"The Perfect Inn on 9th street, room 307."

"Be ready."

"Yes Mommy."

She did not remember putting her things into the little overnight bag she'd purchased earlier in the day; nor did she remember checking out of the hotel. However, she did remember the look on her mother's face when she drove up to the revolving glass doors. Neither of them said a word during the twenty-five minutes it took to cross from the North side of town to the West side where Johanna Hemsley had purchased a four bedroom home thirteen months earlier. She'd returned to San Antonio to be with the family God had given to her an eighty pounds much lighter Johanna. She'd taken the early retirement, sold her home, and said good-bye to her church family. All in time to become the nanny grandmother so her one and only daughter could return to the corporate rat race.

Hannah wasn't concerned about leaving her car parked at the hotel. She just wanted a safe familiar place to be at that point in time. The crescent moon was playing peek-a-boo with the clouds when they drove down the long driveway to her Mother's house. Stars weren't big or bright that night but barely visible in the mystical Texas sky. It looked about as bleak as her future.

"You can stay here as long as you need too Baby Girl" her mother said before taking her sleeping granddaughter. Instead of putting her to bed she sat her on her lap and began rocking the already napping Joy back and forth. Hannah did not know what to make of her. She felt guilty for including her mother in her distasteful affairs but she and Joy needed her. This time she was not going to pretend she could come through yet another storm in life alone. As fate would have it she was home.

Chapter 5

On Sunday she did not make an appearance at Grace Church. Nor did she allow her mother to take Joy with her. It didn't make her mother happy, but it wasn't her decision to make. It wasn't that she was uninterested in hearing from God; she did not want the son of Satan greeting them at the door like they were the perfect family. She couldn't trust herself. During the night she had plotted his murder, set their house on fire, and beat him to death. Which one, if any, of those criminal acts she could actually carry out she wasn't certain. She just knew it would not be polite to commit murder in the house of God. She was still in a world wind of emotions and morning sickness. Her heart and her gut felt like they were taking a leave of absence from her body and no amount of talking could convince them to stay. The battle from their duel gave her a permanent headache.

By the following Saturday she knew she would have to tell those closest to her that she and Brice had split and that alone had sucked the remaining life she had left right out of her. Jane was angry; no surprise. Tobias and Kelly prayerful, her mother was still gravely disappointed but she refused to bad mouth him. Michael wanted to get in his car with his boys and teach Brice a lesson. He was the only one of which she shared all of the gruesome details. She knew her mother should be spared those kinds of images. After hearing or rather not hearing him on the other end of the phone she knew she had made a terrible choice. When Michael James was quiet, trouble was always sure to follow. He loved hard and he loved long, but when you crossed him, there would be no reconciliation. To Michael, Brice had crossed the line when he hurt his sister and that was taboo. Even across the many miles from Texas to Washington their friendship was stronger than ever. He was over protective and Hannah was somewhat nervous about what he would do. She confided in him because he was easy to talk to and would take her secrets to the grave with him. Now what his next move would be concerning Brice was something else for her to worry about.

The pregnancy was still between her and God alone; Michael being the only exception. The timing was all wrong, but she was having a baby and was happy about it. Maybe the life inside of her was her sign from God that she could rebuild her life once more as a single parent. It wasn't planned but the little baby would be welcomed with all her heart. She would go on with her life and raise her children alone. She had a good job, a nice little nest egg, and a pretty good support system; they would be just fine. She had to figure out if she would remain in her mother's home or find an apartment of her own. The only thing she was changing concerning Joy was the one day a week music class. She couldn't take a chance on him picking her up from the school or pulling some kind of stunt. Johanna would watch her on Wednesdays until she figured something out. Brice dared not face her mother. Her disappointment in him would be too much so Joy was safe.

Wanting to do something routine for Joy's sake, mother and daughter had a tea party in her special bedroom at her grandmother's house. It was hard to smile when she wanted to crawl into the bed and cry, but for her daughter's sake she would not. After lunch, Miss Summer Anna-Joy, almost two but going on forty-two, was all puckered out and took her regularly scheduled nap in the princess bed her grandmother insisted she have. Hannah lay on the plush carpet beside her bed. Feeling the phone vibrate in her pocket, her intention was to identify the caller, but somehow she hit the accept button in the process. Relief flooded her mind when it turned out to be Ian.

"Hello."

"Hi Curly Sue. How are you holding up?"

"Hi Ian, I guess you heard?"

"Yup I did. I was hoping that it was just a rumor."

"Depends on what you heard."

"Well according to what my step-mother told my father, you left your husband because you didn't want to be married anymore."

"That sounds like something she would say."

"Exactly. That is why I am calling you. Not to get in your business but to let you know that I realize it is a lot more to the story and I love you and I sincerely want you and my brother to make it."

"This was all his doing. He found someone else so I don't think that will be happening. I see a lawyer on Monday."

"Wow, so soon. Give yourselves some time to cool off and then try coming together to see if you can at least try and save your marriage."

"He committed adultery Ian. Not just that but he admitted she makes him happy, not me."

"Brice is gullible Hannah. He was caught in the web of lust."

"So you are trying to tell me he is the victim here?"

"No, but what I am saying is that he is not used to other women paying him that much attention. He doesn't know that he isn't the only one and it is just a game to see what happy home they can destroy."

"I don't buy it Ian. He is responsible for his own actions. He didn't have to create the secret account. He didn't have to go to the hotel sometimes on a weekly basis. He didn't have to lie to me about working late and spend our money buying her things."

"All I am saying is do not be so quick to run off to divorce court Curly Sue. Give it time."

"No Ian, I gave him everything I had and it wasn't enough. He said so himself. He said he needed more and so I am just going to give him all the opportunity he needs to go out and get it legally."

"Do you remember when we first met?"

"What does that have to do with anything?"

"Do you?"

"How could I forget? You didn't look like any minister to me. At first I thought Brice had hired someone to pose as a preacher just so we could get married."

Ian laughed and little does he know it was like putting a knife to her heart. He sounded like her husband. The cheating, lying, good for nothing, man who had broken her heart just like everyone else. The husband that was the greatest father in the world that she couldn't convince her heart to stop loving. Over and over again she asked herself, "How can you love a cheater and a deceiver?" but her heart had no answer besides pain.

"Oh yeah I remember those looks you gave me. I kept praying Lord don't allow this pregnant woman to beat me up."

She laughed out loud for the first time in days. "Now the truth comes out."

"It always does, eventually."

"I guess it will." Her mind wandered until he began speaking again.

"I remember the way the two of you looked at each other. How protective Brice was of you and your baby. How he fought his parents tooth and nail to make you his wife. The things he willingly gave up. He loved you then Hannah Chandler and I know he loves you now. He may have made some detrimental choices but he still loves you. I would bet money on it."

Trying to make light of the situation she says, "So my family now consist of a gambling minister and a cheating husband."

"Watch it Curly" he says, taking her lead. "The Chandler men may be a piece of work at times, but we find our way in due course."

"What makes you so sure he still loves me? How could he love me and do such things?"

"He would have left on his own. He wouldn't have waited to be caught. Now you and I both know Brice is an expert when it comes to computers. You would never have been able to find anything. Plus he left a trail with the bank account."

"Maybe that was all a part of God's plan to show me who I married."

"You know who you married Hannah. You knew just who he was when you came all the way back from Washington. You knew what kind of heart he had and it was just what you wanted and needed. Can you be what he needs you to be now? Don't give up on him Hannah."

"Ian I've grown weary of fighting for his attention and begging for his time. I'm going to play the hand I was dealt and it looks like divorce is my only trump card."

"You wouldn't be so anxious to play it if you knew who had actually dealt you that hand."

"It's just so much. I don't know what to do."

"Start with forgiving him and then move forward from there."

"I don't think I can forgive him."

"Just ask God to help you and He will. Have the two of you spoken since you left?"

"No, I haven't taken any of his calls."

"Maybe I'd better check on him then. Curly Sue…don't think you are alone in this."

"Thanks Ian."

"Goodbye Sis."

When her mother returned from church, mother and daughter were fast asleep in the pink and purple room.

Chapter 6

The smell of peach cobbler woke her from the coma like sleep. How long she'd slept she wasn't certain. She got a good idea when she entered the living room and Joy ran to her yelling, "Mommy! Mommy! I so missed you!" There was nothing like her hugs and kisses. They spent a few minutes cuddling before hunger pains got the better of her. Today she actually had an appetite and she intended to make full use of it. She hastily ran to the sink to wash her hands and served herself a big helping of homemade peach cobbler with a hefty scoop of vanilla ice cream.

"Well hello to you too Hannah Renee!"

"I'm sorry Mommy," she said kissing her on the cheek. "Thank you for watching Joy while I slept and thank you for this peach cobbler."

Laughing she shook her head in a motherly fashion. "I aim to please."

"Well I thank you and my stomach thanks you. How was church Mommy?"

"Church was wonderful. It would have been nice to have you there with me, but I understand why you didn't come."

"What did Reverend Wilson have to say today? And did Ms. Lucy shout her hat off again today?"

"Do not get me started. You already know the answer to one of those questions. That hat fell off with the wig in it."

They both laughed so hard little Joy comes over and join them having no idea what they were so giddy about. Seeing her bounce up and down and slap her leg just like her father almost startled Hannah. She was so much like Brice it was frightening.

"There is but one Lucy Mae Fritters. Lord have mercy on us all, especially poor Reverend Wilson. He couldn't get his composure back after that wig incident."

"No!!!"

"He had to lean over the podium. The church went into an uproar because they thought God was moving on him. But they didn't see that hat fly off her head with the wig in it and they certainly did not see Sister Cheryl do the mash potato all over it. I tried to get over there and save it but I was too late. That hair was dead before she brought it to church anyway. Some people need to have a sign and today I think Lucy got one. I had to take one of those sheets and wrap her up like a nun and walk her out of church because that real hair looked like the bride of Frankenstein."

"Mommy!! Stop! You are making my stomach hurt."

"No my child, if I had to endure it, you will most certainly hear about it. She cried all the way to the restroom moaning about that being a family air loom. Her grandmother gave it to her mother and her mother left it to her. Now what kind of foolishness is that? Money, homes, values, that's what your ancestors should leave you. Not bad hair. That is not God."

"Say it is not so Mommy!"

"Now you know I speak the truth. Everything was a bit off today. All the altar workers caught it. Beverly was hit in the eye. Sister Hinton tripped over that long maxi dress she likes to wear and Matilda lost her slip. Somebody is not praying because I know God is not the author of confusion. By the end of the service three people were in the nurses' station. Pace maker gone mad, near foot crushing and Mr. Solomon needed an extra nerve pill. Apparently, Mrs. Solomon, age eighty-five, is pregnant with the new Pope. "

It took a good long while for Hannah to stop laughing. Her mother was glad to see her with some joy if only for a brief moment. She studied her daughter; so much pain, so much trouble in her young life. It wasn't up to her to question God but there were so many things she did not understand. She just wanted her to be happy, safe, and to hold on to her faith in God. Now all of that was being tested. Once again her baby was in a crisis, but her worse fears were that this was only the beginning of her sorrows.

They made small talk and watched cartoons with Joy until Hannah suddenly became ill. Jumping up from the chase she sprinted to the trash can in the kitchen because it is closest. With regret she lost every bit of peach cobbler she'd scarf down. Recovery took some time because evidently her stomach was angry with everything she'd eaten in the past couple of days. All she had strength left to do was lay sprawled out on the cold kitchen floor after the episode was over. She wanted to get up and take out the trash. She wanted to console Joy who must be frightened and she wanted to get up and splash her face with cold water. All of those things were mere wishes and at that moment were as impossible as having a snow storm in July in the Longhorn state.

She welcomed the cool towel her mother laid on her face. Whispering a barely audible, "Thank you," she promised to take out the trash in a few minutes.

"No I have it baby you just rest."

By now Joy was laying on the floor next to her looking in her face making sure she was okay.

"Mommy okay? Mommy okay?" her voice sounded nervous.

For that reason she forced herself up, took out the trash, gave her daughter a bath and put her to bed before she collapsed on the couch in the living room. When she returned her mother had put away the food and tidied up the kitchen and living room and was rocking in her recliner. Neither of them said anything for an entire sitcom. Johanna finally broke the silence.

"How far along are you?"

Hannah wondered how she could go straight to her being pregnant. She really did not want to talk about it yet, but she guessed destiny would have it that way.

"I don't know. It wasn't planned."

"Maybe it was just a part of God's plan. When do you plan on finding out?"

She shrugged her shoulder, "I don't know."

"You don't have anything to be ashamed of Baby Girl. You haven't done anything wrong. Now I know it, but you need to know it too."

"Yes Ma'am."

"Does Brice know?"

"No Ma'am, only Michael."

"You and that child always were inseparable. How is he?"

"Violent."

"Can't say I blame him for that one; it's a praying time baby."

She did not reply to her mother's response. She knew her well enough to understand that it required no answer. She was rocking in her chair quietly humming a tune she didn't recognize and reading her Bible. Hannah welcomed the quietness to her troubled soul. They both had a lot on their minds.

About an hour or so later her mother got up from her chair, covered her daughter with one of her special quilts, the ones with the scriptures written all over them, and kissed her good night. Before she left the room she said, "Tomorrow you aren't seeing a lawyer you're seeing a doctor."

"Yes Ma'am" was all she answered.

By Monday evening a husband wasn't the only thing she was about to lose. Obviously, her job was up for grabs. Their contractor merged with another contractor and apparently her services were no longer needed at the Lyndell Corporation. She knew going in the job would not last forever, but she still hoped it would. If only employment was the only problem she had. The pregnancy was already giving her complications. They diagnosed her as high risk right from the start and she was placed on bed rest for the remainder of the week. Her blood pressure was too high, iron levels too low and she had a cyst, the source of her pain, and it was life threatening to the baby. Her mother held her hand during the entire doctor's visit.

Up until this point she had not done much crying but on that Monday evening she had a severe case of the blues. Retreating to her mother's prayer room she laid on the floor and instead of having a little talk with Jesus, she had a bona fide crying session. She could not believe how suddenly life could change. Her life went from having a little rain in it to being in a full-fledged tornado. Giving up was not an option for her, but she knew without God's help and strength she would never make it. This was the first battle she'd had to fight without her husband at her side. He was there when she walked through the ordeal with Miss. Ann. He was there when his mother allowed her mean streak to get the best of her and took it out on her. He was there when little Joy was hospitalized the first time, the second time, and the third time. That first year was full of ups and downs with her food allergies, coughs, fevers and bugs. He always held her hand, talked her through it, and prayed them out of it. She missed him immensely until she remembered the woman. Then she remembered little Joy, then her current job situation, and the little baby growing inside her and the crying started all over again.

When she felt her mother put her hand on her back and caressed it in circle like motions she didn't know what to think. Comfort seemed so far away from her at that point.

"Come on Baby Girl, let's get you to bed. Things always feel better after a good night's sleep and a good cry."

She did not argue, just got up and walked to Joy's room and got in the full size bed with her. She needed to be close to her baby.

Chapter 7

On Wednesday her mother went bowling with her ladies group and Jane spent the day with Hannah. Convincing her mother that she did not need to be baby sat was pointless. Her mother was well aware that Jane played Bingo on Wednesday's and then visited her Grand Ma Ma who was now in an elderly care home, but they'd both double teamed her. It wasn't her friend and sister missing out on her gambling that concerned her. It was Grand Ma Ma not seeing her that day. Each person in their family had a day to make sure the people in her facility did what they were supposed to do and Wednesday was Jane's turn. None of the family wanted her in a home but she had insisted it was right for her at this time in her life and reluctantly they had agreed.

Hannah was finding it hard to stay focused and she was sure she was not good company. They made small talk and watched little Joy play most of the morning. The scene was much like one she'd lived out before. The two sat on the deck while Joy played in her doll house. Just a little more than two years ago they were doing the same thing but it was Jane's house and little R. J. playing. The very day she told her sister friend that she was going to marry Brice and would be moving out to be with him. She wondered over and over what she had missed with her husband. What signs did she not heed? Why did life have to be so hard? Was there ever going to be a time in her life when she could hang up her boxing gloves?

"Girl stop it!"

"What Jane! You are starting to annoy me already." She was feeling irritable with pregnancy hormones, grief and heartache and the fact that Jane could read her every mood just plain annoyed her.

"Stop worrying because you are going to make yourself sick and then I'm going to get angry and that is going to make me have to visit Ms. Cleopatra down on Perry and Blake and have her make me a doll just for him so I can stick it to him."

"Now Jane, you should be ashamed of yourself. What would God think of that?"

"I want to know what He thinks of Brice sticking Mr. Happy where it didn't belong."

"God had nothing to do with that. People make choices and that was his choice."

"Well I choose to make him a special dish that will make you rich in thirty-six hours, guaranteed."

"Like he would ever eat it. You know he always thought you were a little crazy."

"He would be right to think that. That scoundrel better watch his back."

Hannah really did not know what to feel for Brice. Some days she hated his very guts and others she just missed her husband and best friend. Was it fair to hate him because he'd moved on? He still provided for them. He was still a great father. He just no longer wanted her. Did that warrant punishing him and keeping him from Joy? Getting weary of talking and thinking about Brice almighty Hannah changed the subject.

"Forget Brice. What's going on with you missy? Don't think I haven't seen the way you've been waltzing around here lately. Checking your phone every few minutes and smiling like a Cheshire Cat. Who is he Missy Lou?"

Batting her eyes mischievously she says, "Now Han, whatever do you mean? I haven't the faintest idea as to what you are talking about."

"Liar! Please don't play innocent with me. Acting was never your strong point."

"Well, since you asked, girl…he's that scrumptious parking lot attendant at your church."

"Oh my goodness! Is that why you have been going to church? Silly me thinking it was Jesus."

"See that's why I didn't tell you. I know how you act all holy trying to make me look like a heathen. I can't help it if the man is drop dead gorgeous and I just happen to be single, sexy, and unsatisfied. Anyway, how do you know seeing him that very day was not how it was meant to be. I mean it was raining and all and I had to get real close under that umbrella to stay dry. Seeing how we were already close I didn't think there was anything wrong with me whispering my phone number to him. I saw it as a public service."

"Only you would. And for your social calendar I don't act holy, I go to church because I'm trying to learn how to live right."

"Excuse me Sister Mary Catherine but I need a man and they have them at your church. Any kind I want. Sexy, good looking, Sugar daddy, Big daddy, young, old, short, tall, fat, skinny, black, white, Hispanic, African, Asian, and other."

"Other Jane." Chuckling too herself a bit Hannah added, "I can see you are up on your manology. Just how long has this been going on Jennifer?"

"You would be right. It's been long enough for me to rock his world a couple three times."

"Just ratchet!"

"Girl I have needs. A year and a half is a long time. Even the men at the nursing home were starting to look good."

"My my my aren't you scandalous!"

"Don't judge me. I mean I can work with a walker and a wheel chair. I'm creative like that."

By now Hannah can no longer stifle her laughs. "Oh I'm not judging my sister, just amazed is all. Now you know I have to know…how was he?"

"Had me singing soprano and you know I am a TENOR!"

"That good huh?"

"No, better. Much much better."

True to her hormonal hurricane, Hannah's mood changes from the playful manner. "Just be careful okay Jane."

"Oh Han I'm so sorry. I didn't mean to be insensitive."

"Oh please Jane. I'm fine. Looking forward to the next phase of my life."

"Knock, knock, did you forget who you were talking to? As much as I want to go upside his head I know you still love him."

"Love has nothing to do with this Jane."

"Yes it does. It has everything to do with it. If you didn't love him it wouldn't hurt so much. You wouldn't be ten pounds lighter and a thousand pounds heavier. Brice was the perfect guy. He was one of the good ones. If the Brice's of the world can't make it what hope do any of us have?"

"I feel like such a fool. I have all these images running through my head that make me sick every time I think about it. I trusted him with everything."

"What are you going to do? You know I'm behind you every step of the way whatever your decision."

"Divorce is the only choice for me."

"Oh Han. I've been down that road before. I pray you try to avoid it if at all possible."

"Do you regret leaving Robert?"

"No, what I regret is knowing that I did not do everything in my power to make it work before I gave up on him and our marriage. In this life anything you get you will have to fight to keep. I don't think I was as willing to fight to make it work as I was to get out of it. The truth is Han, although he is married again, if I called him today he would come running and I know it. I refuse to be that woman."

For a while they sat together on the red leather couch head to head and holding hands.

"I'm pregnant Jane."

It isn't Hannah that cried this time. It is Jane. She knows how much pain her friend is in, she could feel it, and it just hurt too much. When she touched her friend she felt like she was in a black hole and it was sucking all the life out of her. Why did some people catch more hell than others? How was it that those who don't deserve it go through such awful things while others lead carefree lives? Had it been possible to take her pain she would have. How she wished it were possible.

After getting herself together Jane goes into full protective mode. It was weird how when Jane became upset her Cajun accent went into full force. Sometimes you had to really think about what she was saying and other times you just knew whatever she said was not English and left it at that. This was one of those times.

"O chile, My poor bebe. Don't you worry Sis things are going to work out. Remember what that preacher man told you that time."

By now Hannah was exhausted and still dealing with the pain in her abdomen area. She was following doctor's orders to the letter. What she hadn't told anyone was that she had begun spotting.

"Do you mind if I take a nap? At least before your niece gets up ready to paint the town pink and purple."

"Don't you worry about me or my niece. If she wakes up while you're resting we are going to have some quality time together. I get to play dress up girl; you know that little woman has fashion sense already."

"We know who to fault for that one…" At the same time they both say, "Her daddy!"

"Thanks Jane."

"Please. You just rest now." With that Jane left the room, but not before kissing her on the forehead.

Just before drifting off to sleep she sees her phone light up with a message from Brice that said, "Talk to me please. I'll give anything to have my family back."

Chapter 8

All week long Hannah's dreams had been dismal. If she wasn't running she was fighting; if not fighting, she was drowning; if not drowning she was ill. Taking full advantage of the medicine the doctor prescribed to calm her she slept a lot but was still tired. Praying was what she'd done more than anything but she didn't know if her prayers were working judging from the current events in her life. She loved Johanna and did not know what she would do without her love and support; but she was longing for the only mother she'd known and loved until she was taken away from her so suddenly. She often wondered what she would think of her life had she still been alive. It probably was not a smart thought pattern because she knew most of her tragedies would not have occurred had her mother still been alive. There was no element of surprise when her doctor's appointment did not bring good news. The old fear and depression were no surprise either. So were the chapters of Hannah Renee's life.

According to the doctor the fate of her pregnancy was all up to nature. Before she could respond to him her mother had already shot him down with, "No not nature, God would be the one in control of this situation." The doctor only nods his head and continues speaking to her, "Many women spot and even have normal periods during pregnancy, but you are losing more blood than I'd like to see and your tests concern me a bit. My concern is that you may be threatening a miscarriage. At this point all we can do is wait and hope. I'd like to do more labs today to give me a better idea as to what is actually going on." The bad news just continued to come.

By the following week Hannah had been forced to purchase half a wardrobe for herself. Besides her own bedroom, castle outside, and ridiculous play toys, Joy had a second wardrobe at her grandmother's house already and for the first time Hannah actually appreciated that fact. They were still in limbo. Brice was still being ignored and she could feel some tension arising between her and her mother because of it. What was she supposed to say to her cheating husband anyway? What she wanted to say to him was not what Jesus would say she already knew that. How was saying I'm sorry I had a good time putting Mr. Winkie where it didn't belong until I was caught going to help anything? No, she was certain they had nothing to discuss; including Joy.

When week three rolled around her mother's prayer team had grown weary, restless, and worn. Some were just plain tired from trying to figure out why Sister Jo's daughter was living at home and not with her husband. Others wanted to know why Sister Hannah stayed in bed all the time. The rest just wanted to do a mighty work for the Lord and on one particular Wednesday they got their chance.

"Sister Jo, I really feel like we need to pray for your daughter," begged Sister Emma formerly of the professional mourners of Ziton. The ones dating back five generations to the lineage of the slave that lost his foot in the fight for freedom and she had the papers to prove it, was certain it was Hannah's time to be freed. It didn't take much for the rest of the group to agree. Thus, Hannah Renee was summoned to the prayer circle of deliverance. Of course they were kind enough to allow her to sit down. So kind of them to make sure her chair was directly in the middle of their wailing and wooing about poor Sister Hannah's troubles. Someone poured oil in her hair, on her hands and then her feet. Sister Dempsey poured some oil in her own hands first, rubbed them together vigorously, and then slapped poor Sister Hannah upside the head so hard she was sure she saw the light for a second or two.

Sister Mackey, who apparently had undiagnosed hearing lost, so she always talked extremely loud, ran in the middle of the circle and screamed, "Let it go child!" Besides spitting in her face, Hannah was sure her breathe could have been used to fight chemical warfare. Flinching, she doubled over to take cover just in case there was going to be another shower. The group supposed she was being touched and became overly excited. Some were singing old hymns, others humming, and the rest were praying. They clapped, stomped, and played the tambourine. Hannah was relieved that Jane had taken little Joy on a play date with R.J. because she was sure their meeting might have been a traumatic moment in her little childhood. By now Hannah felt a hand on her back patting her as if she were choking. Someone else was rubbing her feet of which she was very ticklish and this caused her to slide to the floor. Her body was now shaking and her face to the floor buried in the carpet. All she could see were feet, open toed shoes, and flower printed dresses. "Oh baby it's okay, you just let it go" someone said. She couldn't tell who because she was laughing so hard her body continued to convulse. That's when Clarese has a fainting spell, which makes her twin sister, Marese very upset. "Oh sister, sister come back to me" she pleaded. Mrs. Cassie, who did not play, not even with the Lord Jesus Himself, was not in the mood and took a handkerchief and popped Clarese with it and said, "Get up! Right now I say, get up!" Just like Clarese had fallen she made a remarkable recovery. "Now go sit down somewhere until it's time to go. I swear I can't take you anywhere!" she scolded them. This caused Hannah to laugh even more until tears are running down her face as fast as the oil that had been thrown on her head. She laid there, her mouth covered, tears falling on the shoe Clarese has left behind in her speedy deliverance; making sounds that no one could decipher. That was a good thing.

When it was all over she practically glided to her room, thanks to the oil change she'd been given. Truth be told she did feel somewhat better. Maybe it was because she had laughed until she forgot about all of her sorrows. Perhaps it was all the bear hugs, foot rubs, and feeling the kisses of pure gums. Then it could have just been the prayer alone. As she glided back to the bed she was a little more positive then she had been since all of the details of her life had become a public matter.

That afternoon she decided to talk to her brother. His cancer was still in remission and his life was back to normal, at least the new normal after having been so close to death that he'd lived in that world more than this present one. There was always something comforting about the way he spoke to her. She needed that something.

"Hi T."

"How is my Hannah Banana?"

"Fine. Just calling to say hello."

"That good aye?"

"Whatever could you mean? Can't a sister call just because she wants to hear her brother's voice?"

"Most assuredly she can and her brother will always be elated to hear from his favorite sister."

"I'm your only sister" she said with faked sarcasm.

"And the best in the world I must say."

"You only say that because you know I could take you if I wanted to."

"Lord please do not let Hannah want to" he prayed playfully.

"Not fair, you're not supposed to seek divine intervention on me now."

"Yes it is fair when you need it."

He smiled on the other end of the phone. She could tell because it warmed her insides. That had been the very reason she'd called. He always saw light regardless of the darkness. Closing her eyes, she lay back on her pillow and coveted the moment.

He continued, "I'm not ashamed to admit my sister can bully me. I love her just the same."

"What other choice do you have?"

"See, bully! Just like I said and you and God already knew. Now, how is my little sister doing? The truth this time."

"Don't know T. Just can't get out of the darkness this time. Sometimes it's hard to even talk to God."

"Maybe He isn't the one you should be speaking to?"

"How is that possible?"

"Many times we hide behind God knowing we should be speaking to others. Have you spoken to Brice?"

"Just can't. The sound of his name makes me sick. His voice would be worse I'm sure."

"That is a possibility but maybe it may make you better. Talking may take some of the pain of not knowing away."

"All the information I need I already have. He is a cheater, a deceiver, a liar and I hate him."

"And you love him, miss him, need him, and want him. Plus you're scared and you want permission to forgive him if he gives you a good enough reason to because you want your family."

That was all it took for her to start weeping, again. "Today is our second anniversary. He sent flowers and I threw them out. How could I still love him?"

"Because your heart is not a faucet and you just can't turn it off. I am willing to bet he loves you too little sister. I've seen the way he looks at you. The way he has to touch you. The way he tries so hard to make your every wish come true."

"Then why did he do it?"

"Only he can answer that, but I am sure he had some outside help."

"Doubt it."

"How does first class round trip tickets to good old Richmond sound for you and Joy. I know Kelly and Ally would find a thousand things for the four of you to get into?"

"No can do. Doctor's orders, I am officially on bed rest."

"What doctor? When and for what reason and why am I just hearing about it.?"

"Didn't want to worry you T."

"You're my family Hannah Banana. No worries, just concerns. Now why are you on bed rest?"

The Medical Doctor in him had stepped up and taken charge. Hannah knew she must not leave out one detail or she would not be allowed to hang up the phone or change the subject. So the next hour was spent filling him in on the pregnancy, the cyst, the complications, and her filing divorce papers and not telling anyone. He would not judge her, but he would give her sound advice when she was ready to hear it. They both knew now was not the time to lecture or condemn, but to listen and be the friend she needed so desperately. So he just loved on her a little bit and assured her that his shoulder was there and his doors were open and he would be checking in on her very often. She needed to know she had some place to run should she need to take flight and that provided some comfort to her.

Chapter 9

When her mother came in with the mail one evening Hannah was surprised that she gave her an envelope. Emotion almost slapped her senseless when she recognized the hand writing. Now why would Brice write her at her mother's residence? Her thoughts were so wicked in that moment she wanted to blame them on the devil but she knew that she alone was responsible. She wasn't the only one that recognized the hand writing, Johanna Hemsley missed nothing.

"Who is the prettiest girl in the world?"

"Me me me!" Joy responded to her grandmother's question jumping up and down.

"Then how about the prettiest girl in the world come and bake cookies with me?"

"Woo hoo!" An overzealous Joy ran ahead of her grandmother to the kitchen. Hannah and her mother shook their heads at the latest addition to her vocabulary. Who knew where she got it, but each week she was learning something different. When they headed for the kitchen Hannah knew exactly what her mother was doing and was grateful. Walking outside, she sat at the picnic table in the back yard for a minute. It was mid July and hot as could be. The breeze brought no relief to the hot dry atmosphere. Although the sun had set it was still sweltering. The neighbor's children two houses down were playing in the pool in their backyard. The sounds of the their voices laughing and yelling while splashing in the pool was heard not just by Hannah but the dog next door was protesting rather rudely about it. This made its owner repeatedly yell, "shut up Ju Ju!" Only Ju Ju was not in compliance. The sound of the ice cream truck coming down the street further added to his annoyance and he started to howl at the music.

After the children went inside, the dog stopped barking, and the street lights came on she opened the envelope. Not wanting to read the letter in her husband's handwriting that lay on top of a stack of papers she flipped the page and realized that he had returned their divorce papers, unsigned. It angered her. Why? What was the hold up? He had done his thing and now she must do hers. She took out her phone and dialed his numbered.

"Hello…"

"You asinine, trifling, excuse for a man. How dare you not sign the divorce papers? Isn't this what you wanted? You had to know it would come to this. Give me back my life so I can start over. Or I will make sure you never see Joy again Brice Anthony Chandler and you know I will do it!"

"I'll just have to take that chance then."

That shocked her like having cold water thrown in your face kind of thing. She was incapable of reading his mood and so she went on with her insults. "So it's that easy for you to give her up? I guess you've had enough of playing daddy. Good, because I will find her another one. It won't be difficult to do because you all are brainless, spineless, heartless carcasses who think with your anatomy and don't give a crap about anyone else."

"Everything you say about me is true and probably so much more. What I did to you, to Joy, to us was wrong and I don't know if I will ever be able to make it right, but I refuse to give up the chance to try."

"Try what Brice? You can't fix this. Nothing and no one can fix this and even if they could I don't know if I would want them to."

"Please forgive me Han. You are the love of my life and I know I broke your heart and disappointed you and I don't deserve your forgiveness but I beg you for it anyway."

"How could you Brice? What if I cheated on you? Let's say I slept with Connor. If I just couldn't resist that tall gorgeous perfectly tanned 6'2 body? If I found his curly red hair too irresistible and I just had to have him sex me up just one more time? Would you be so willing to just forgive me?"

Silence followed. She heard him grinding his teeth and was sorry she had hit below the belt but felt he deserved it anyway. She wouldn't let up, "Would you Brice? What if I took Joy to see him and decided I wanted us to be a family because I remembered how great our love making was and how I missed him touching me in all the right places and the way he made me scream his name even when I didn't want to? Could you just forgive me and just say come home Hannah and I will forget all about it and we can start over? Could you Brice?"

She heard him curse and then yell, "No" so loud it hurt her ears. "No one gets the right to touch you like that but me Han. You're MY wife."

"Just like you were supposed to be my husband, my protector, my friend, my secret keeper, my forever love. You promised to teach me about God. You said you would always be there for me and our daughter but you broke your covenant." With that the tears start flowing. The deep silent cry that had gripped her soul escaped and it broke both their hearts. She knew he was crying on the other end of the phone and the crickets, lightening bugs, and mosquitoes knew she was distraught. So did her mother who was watching from the kitchen window. "You were supposed to be a safe place Brice, so I gave you all the love I had, and you trampled it like a useless piece of trash. Please Brice, I want out. Just sign the papers. This wasn't meant to be. Maybe she was the wife you were suppose to have all the time. I just got in the way."

"You're my wife, my love, you really are, I was just stupid. I love you Han. I've never loved anyone but you and I am nothing without you."

"I can't do this Brice. I just can't, it's too much. I have to go."

"Do you still love me Han?"

"Stop Brice. How dare you. How selfish can you be?"

"You are the love of my life. I just wanted you to know."

"Know what? Why are you trying to lay a guilt trip on me? You did this not me."

"That's not what I'm doing at all. My job is sending me to Italy for a couple of months for training. Just wanted you to know that I didn't change anything and if you want to stay at home while I'm not there…"

"That's not my home anymore."

"Well I paid all the bills and put some money in your account. I know you don't want me too but tomorrow I am going to see my daughter. If you aren't there I will wait until you are. I can't allow her to believe that I just don't care about her. Our baby is turning two while I'm gone and I want her to have one of her gifts before I leave."

"Why are you doing this Brice? Can't you just leave it alone?"

"She's my little girl and she can't pay for what I did. I will see her tomorrow?"

"Good-bye Brice."

That night everyone was restless. Hannah lay awake for hours. Joy tossed and turned and Johanna walked and prayed more than she had in a long time. Across town in the ranch style house with the black shutters, with the yellow rose garden and fountain on the front lawn Brice Chandler sat starting at the picture of his wife and daughter wondering if restoring his family would ever be a reality.

When Hannah opened the door the next afternoon a disheveled Brice stood before her. Mr. Neat freak, suit and tie, match and color coordinate everything looked like he was a vagabond. Part of her wanted to comfort him, console him. The other part wanted to beat the living crap out of him. Before she had a chance to figure out which one she would adhere to Joy spotted her daddy standing in the doorway.

"Daddy, daddy, daddy!! My daddy's here! My daddy!" She ran straight into his arms and burst into tears. The scene sent Hannah running from the room. She cried as well. What had she done to her little girl?

Thirty minutes passed and there was a tap on the door. Wiping her face Hannah gets up in response to it. Brice was standing there with his daughter in his arms. "May I please take her to play outside?" Seeing the two of them together she knew it would have taken nothing short of death to pull them apart.

"She has to have her sun block and bug repellant first." As she turned to retrieve the items she hears Brice exhale. The rest of the afternoon and better part of the evening was spent swinging, running, jumping, laughing, playing, tickling, hugging, kissing, wrestling, rocking, consoling, and holding time for the two. Joy received a shiny red tricycle and wagon for her upcoming birthday and the two put them both to good use.

Hannah was exhausted and ready for an early night. She become livid when her mother invited her estranged husband to stay for dinner. She openly and boldly rolled her eyes and went to Joy's room deciding to skip dinner altogether. Brice wasn't detoured. He stayed on with his daughter for a while. After reading her favorite story for the tenth time, he bathed her, then sat for a while watching television with her and Johanna until little Joy fell asleep in his arms. That's when he knocked on the door to put her to bed. Hannah was too tired to get up. She was bleeding again. When she said "Come in" Brice opened the door and lay his daughter down on the opposite side of the bed and kissed her goodnight. It surprised Hannah when he came to where she lay in the bed and kissed her goodnight too.

"I love you Hannah Renee Chandler and I always will." Her heart whispered, "I love you too" but he never heard it. He'd left the room. She wanted to call out to him to stay but she was afraid to move. Maybe it was because she was troubled that the doctor was right about the baby. He had been her rock through her pregnancy with little Joy and she wished things could be the same with this baby. She knew they would not be.

Chapter 10

As Hannah lay in the bed curled in a fetal position she longed for the doctor to give her something to help her disengage with the world. So much pain flooded her soul. Pain she couldn't describe, pain she wished she had never known, pain she wanted to alienate herself from, but its grip was over powering. Crumbling under its blows she gritted her teeth and clenched her hands without realizing it. Her entire world had been infiltrated with pain. With the pain a new question emerged. Why had God taken her baby? Why did He allow such a thing? Why at this time in her life? Rolling over in the hospital bed she mumbled over and over to no one in particular, "I want my baby." Now she had two dead children; one by abortion of her own hand and the other by miscarriage. Or maybe she had done something to kill this baby too. Maybe God had not seen fit to bring another child into a broken home. She longed for Johanna, but knew Joy needed her with Jane being out of town. Brice wasn't an option even if he had been in town. It would have been a conversation she just wasn't strong enough to have at that time.

Her breasts were swollen from preparation to produce the milk that would have nourished her baby. The middle section of her body still gave hint that life was growing inside of her with the small baby bump remaining quite visible. She still craved ice and longed for salty foods. But no desire was greater than the craving she had for her baby. All she longed to do was know her child. Had it been a boy or a girl? Would the baby have been like its Mommy or Daddy? What kinds of food what he or she have favored? What kind of personality would they have had? How would little Joy have responded? Her heart screamed, "God I just want my child back. May I please just have my baby if just for a little while? I just want a chance to get to know my child." In that moment, the place where you would rather die than endure such pain, where you have very little hope at all and despair is common place, where she pleaded to God for the impossible was when she heard it.

"That's how your mother feels."

Without thinking she says is an audible whisper, "My mother is in heaven."

"Yes, Kimberlee is with me, but you still have Angela."

"She could never be my mother."

"She carried you until birth. She did have another choice. She just didn't know how to carry you any further so she found someone she was certain could care for you and love you as you deserved."

"But she already had another chance when I was orphaned and she blew it."

"Now she is ready. She needs you. She needs your forgiveness."

"She doesn't deserve it."

"That isn't your choice. She longs for you like you long for your baby. Can I trust you to be there for her? I will be there with you every step of the way."

"Why God,…why?"

"For you. This is for you Hannah. You will heal as you open your heart and forgive her."

Hannah wrestled with God as though she were in a physical war. "No, I can't, why, please Lord, if you help me, oh God why, I feel like I'm going crazy," until it was just too much for her wearied soul. Maybe her mind was playing tricks on her but she swore she saw other people in the room. Faces flashed here and there, some friendly, smiling, some stern and frightening, others monstrous. There were flashes of light then darkness, peace then turmoil, joy then sorrow. She didn't see her vitals going out of control. Neither did she see the worried look on the faces of the medical staff at the nurses' station. When the doctor sent in a nurse with something to make her sleep; she remained detached. At that point in her life she was doing all she could to keep breathing and even that was becoming a challenge.

When she awakened something was different. The atmosphere in her room was no longer suffocating her. Had she died? Did God take her too?

Then she heard it, the words, the familiar voice; Bob was sitting next to her hospital bed reading the Bible.

"**1** In that day, everyone in the land of Judah will sing this song: Our city is now strong! We are surrounded by the walls of God's salvation. **2** Open the gates to all who are righteous; allow the faithful to enter. **3** You will keep in perfect peace all who trust in you, whose thoughts are fixed on you! **4** Trust in the LORD always, for the LORD GOD is the eternal Rock. **5** He humbles the proud and brings the arrogant city to the dust. Its walls come crashing down! **6** The poor and oppressed trample it underfoot. **7** But for those who are righteous, the path is not steep and rough. You are a God of justice, and you smooth out the road ahead of them. **8** LORD, we love to obey your laws; our heart's desire is to glorify your name. **9** All night long I search for you; earnestly I seek for God. For only when you come to judge the earth will people turn from wickedness and do what is right. **10** Your kindness to the wicked does not make them do good. They keep doing wrong and take no notice of the LORD's majesty. **11** O LORD, they do not listen when you threaten. They do not see your upraised fist. Show them your eagerness to defend your people. Perhaps then they will be ashamed. Let your fire consume your enemies. **12** LORD, you will grant us peace, for all we have accomplished is really from you."

Turning in his direction she half smiled and asked, "Where is that from?"

"Why Ms. Hannah I hope I didn't disturb you. I just felt like it was the right time to read. Hope you don't mind."

"Not at all, it's great to see you Bob."

"Glad to see you Ms. Hannah. I have been praying for you."

"Thank you ever so much Bob. What passage were you reading?"

"That was Isaiah chapter twenty-six Ms. Hannah."

Nodding in response to his answer she closed her eyes again enjoying the peace that has suddenly come to her room. She had no explanation for it. Just that it was like the grief and sorrow, the pain and heartache that had enveloped the room was no longer there. Like something bigger, something greater, something more powerful had come and chased it off.

Bob, who was watching her very closely decided it was now his time to speak. "Ms. Hannah it will be alright. Do you still believe like you use to Ms. Hannah? Please don't give up on Him because He would never give up on you. Trouble don't mean God isn't there it just means you have to fight for what's yours."

"If it's mine then why would I need to fight for it? I can't comprehend that Bob."

"What if someone tried to take that little angel away from you just because they felt like they wanted her more than you?"

"Over my dead body is the only way that is going to happen."

"Then you must have that same fight about this Ms. Hannah. Fight for what's yours."

She knew he was talking about her marriage, her peace, and her life; the good life she was promised.

"Bob…"

"Yes Ms. Hannah."

"How do you know when you have heard from God?"

"Oh you'll know Ms. Hannah, you'll know."

"How Bob? How will I know?"

"Your gut will know. Not your heart because even it can sometimes deceive. You have to also compare it to the Bible. If it is something that directly goes against what it says in His most holy precious Word then don't believe it."

"What if what you heard can't be found in the Bible? At least you haven't seen it yet."

"Everything is in there Ms. Hannah, everything. You must judge if it is going to help. Judge it if it is going to bring healing, even if not at first, but in the long run; if it will do the people involved good, healing, help and freedom, then there is a great chance you heard right."

The two sat pretending to watch the news for the next hour. Their relationship was not understood by most, but they weren't mindful of that. If she had ever had a grandfather she was sure he would have been just like Bob. He was certain she fit into his life just like God planned it before they ever met. Just after sunset the middle-aged 5'9 Caucasian gentle giant made his exit. He hugged her, promised he would be praying for her, then assured her she would be fine, and left the fifth floor of Regional Medical Hospital. She wished he could have stayed longer. Life wasn't so hard when he was in the room. She felt more peaceful and less afraid for her and little Joy's future. He reminded her of the good old days when she and her mother didn't disagree so much. When they enjoyed each other's company more and fought less. When she didn't have to justify her every move, action, decision, and words. She missed her mother, but they too were distant.

So much was always on her mind. She was certain that maybe many of her troubles were because of what she had done to Connor. No matter what took place between the two of them she still knew she'd left wrong. She had no right to take away his little girl or at least the knowledge of her. Guilt about the secrets and the lies plagued her life. She no longer prayed, certain that God was punishing her for something she'd done or maybe not done. The conversation with God, at least she thought it was God, about Miss Ann only added fuel to the fire. How could that situation bring healing to her life when it had been the beginning of all of her pain?

Hannah Renee Corel-Waiters Chandler left the hospital at 3:25p.m., Monday afternoon broken and confused with a hint of bitterness and malice in her heart. Her life was in limbo once again and for someone with her personality that was dangerous. She no longer had a home, a husband, a place of employment, or the unborn baby she longed to have, but she did have two fists full of vengeance and she intended to make Brice feel the brunt of them both. Joy was really her only joy and so for the next few weeks she made her little girl her life. Church was a hit and miss thing pretty much. Every time Johanna asked her about it she just said she didn't feel up to it. That really was the truth. Most days she felt like nothing. That made her isolate herself more and more until one day the walls caved in on her and she picked up the phone.

"Hi there."

"Does that offer still stand?"

"Always. My arms are open wide."

"How does tomorrow sound or is that too soon."

"Tomorrow is great."

"Then we'll be there."

She felt a little better having taken charge of her life again.

Chapter 11

When the bumpy ride came to an end no one was more relieved than Joy. Petrified, she hid her face in her mother's coattail and cried for her daddy for one hour and twenty-three minutes. Hannah's nerves were shot. No amount of prizes, goodies or treats could console her. She wanted off that plane and she wanted her daddy and she did not care who knew. She had not seen him or spoken to him since the day he kissed them goodbye before leaving for Italy. Another lavish birthday gift had arrived right on schedule to her grandmother's house in time for her second birthday. If Hannah did not know any better she was sure Joy was angry with her about not seeing her father. She'd began bed wetting, talking back, and even ignoring her at times. Johanna was now her favorite person in life. She slept with her and played with her, and it broke Hannah's heart. Hannah had her suspicions that Johanna was allowing Joy to speak to her father behind her back. Many clues pointed to that conclusion. Hell would have had to freeze over or her daddy would have to be dead before he would miss speaking to his only daughter on her birthday, yet he had not called her phone. Joy spoke of him more and more and cried a little less at night. Hannah wondered how much of her life Brice knew about. Lately she and her mother had become like oil and water and the weight of it all caused her to run once more.

When the captain gave the all clear to exit the plane Hannah felt like prison doors had just been opened after serving a life sentence. Scooping up her daughter and their things, she sprinted from the airplane like there was a fire. As soon as she entered the lobby she saw him.

"Over here!" waving with excitement he closed the distance between them. His hug was all she'd longed for. "It's so good to see you Sis!"

"You have no idea" she said as he kissed her cheek and took little Joy from her. "Where are Kelly and Ally?"

"Kelly is parked outside and Ally is waiting at home. Let's get your bags so we can get you home. You must be exhausted."

"I'm okay."

"Sure, and I can fly. This is your big brother here remember? You never have to pretend with me."

She knew it was the truth and that made him the safe place she needed. The ride to their home was mostly filled with idle chatter. Joy had crashed and burned and sleeps the entire trip to the suburbs. That was an hour plus tantrum would do for you. Ally was waiting for her little cousin at home with her grandmother. By the time they pulled into the driveway Hannah was ready to join her daughter in la la land. She was beginning to feel the reason her doctor had advised her against traveling so soon after the miscarriage and the surgery that had removed the cyst from her ovaries.

The days that followed were uneventful, slow, and much like heaven to Hannah. Tobias and Kelly did not pressure her about attending church, talking to Brice, or eating. They let her be and that gave her time to rest and her body time to heal. Joy loved having a play mate and the two cousins become instant friends. Ally was all too willing to teach Joy new things and be the leader. So they read books, colored, painted, had tea parties for their dolls, made cookies with granny Milia and played outside. Sometimes all in the same day, but Hannah didn't have to do all of it. There were plenty of hands and loving help as she recuperated.

The plan was for Hannah and Joy to visit for a few days but when she spoke of getting back to San Antonio and not over extending her welcome she could tell that it struck a nerve with Tobias. They'd just finished dinner and the girls had settled down to watch a movie with Kelly's mother. Tobias abruptly left the room and retreated to his study. Kelly gave her the eye to follow him and so she went after him to see just what his problem could be. They were both stubborn and she realized things could get touchy. Not dancing around the subject she got straight to the point. They both preferred it that way.

"What's wrong T?"

"What are you rushing back to Hannah? You need to rest. You have to take care of yourself. I am very concerned about you."

"My reason for coming was not to burden you with my problems."

"What makes you think you are? You're my sister. If you stayed forever I don't believe that would be enough time for us to catch up on all we missed growing up. I hate how it transpired, but I am happy you're here. Besides I know Brice is still in Italy."

"It's not that T, I just need to figure things out. Find my way again."

"Figure what out? Clearing your head so you can make the right decision is what you need to do before you make any rash decisions. Give your body at least couple more weeks to heal before you travel back. You don't have to run anywhere, you are safe here and we want you to stay."

"Are you sure Tobias?"

"As sure as I've ever been about anything."

"Well, I guess I'll be here a little while longer."

"Great. Now get some rest and allow yourself time to heal, doctor's orders."

"Somebody is throwing their weight around again."

"You better believe it."

"Thanks T." With that she walked over and kissed him on the cheek.

"It's all going to work out. Don't worry, just look for the good in the moments of each day you are allowed to see. Count them, breathe them, live them one at a time starting with my beautiful niece. Her silly laugh, pouty lips, her health, that you are reasonably well and capable of making sound decisions. Much of what we take for granted is a miracle for someone else."

Having come back from the grave she had no doubt he knew firsthand the truths he was speaking. When she joined the rest of the family in the living room she knew a little bit of peace had followed her down the hallway. She was grateful that she was able to count many things including the fact that she still had time to get things right with Connor. She had settled it within herself that he must know he had a daughter. The guilt of such a decision to hide Joy from her father had weighed her down far too long.

The following week she spent less time in the upstairs bedroom and more in the family room watching the girls play. She was feeling a little stronger, at least physically, but her mind constantly wondered to her marriage, her daughter, the baby she'd lost, and just how she was going to talk to Connor. Then there was that Johanna thing.

Towards the end of the week Kelly bursts in the room with "good news" and was beside herself with excitement. "He did it! He did it!" Waving an official envelope with a gold seal around Hannah knew what her next line should have been but somehow she knew it might involve her. Her smile was bigger than half the moon and she even did a little dance in her glee. Having never seen the valley girl, who was always so serious, get that much out of character stirred Hannah's curiosity.

Putting her hand in the air Hannah says, "Question over here, who, what, and why?"

"My amazing husband and your brother managed to get his hands on a ticket, only to the event of the year; at least in the tri city medical world."

"Wow that's great." She was happy because it obviously made her sister-in-law a bit giddy. She was almost comical to Hannah.

"Yes it is because this my dear, belongs to you!"

Hannah's mind screams, "Say it's not so!" Apparently her face did also because Kelly started in on her.

"This is just what you need Hannah" her blue eyes were twinkling.

"I can assure you it is not." All Hannah could envision was a room filled with people that were full of themselves. Not her kind of party.

"Oh Hannah it going to be great. Tobias moved heaven and earth to get you this ticket. You just have to go."

"Just when is this evening of elegance going to take place?"

"Saturday! Isn't it awesome?"

"Saturday, as in day after tomorrow Saturday and I have no gown, hair is horrid, nails worse, and you still want me to go Saturday?" Her head instantly began to pound.

"That's the fun of it all. We have an excuse to go shopping and pamper ourselves. Isn't it great?"

Great was unequivocally, without a doubt, most assuredly, not the way she felt about it. Still, after several minutes of saying why she shouldn't go, Kelly gave more reasons why she should. So Hannah, no surprise to anyone, allowed Kelly to convince her to attend a formal benefit to raise cancer awareness and money for the cause. Miss. Omelia agreed to care for the children so they could shop the following afternoon. By the time they left the mall Hannah never wanted to see another for the rest of her life. She was working hard at feeling good about herself again, but she still felt empty and ugly within and without.

The dress she finally chose after her sister-in-law twisted her arm was a size eight and much too revealing for her taste. Kelly argued that she was being way too reserve and modest. With her recent miscarriage and surgery she'd lost about twenty pounds and half of it seemed to go straight to her breast, which made her very self-conscious in the black off shoulder chiffon swing dress. Finding the perfect pair of designer shoes put the icing on the cake for Kelly who was far too excited. Hannah remained bored and exhausted.

Tobias treated them to a spa day in preparation for the gala and Hannah wished it were over before it began. It took her two hours to get up enough nerve to walk out of the bedroom. Her hair wouldn't cooperate, the makeup she wore just didn't apply correctly, the lip gloss was the wrong shade; nothing was right in her eyes. Finally Kelly reached her limit and told her unless she kissed Joy good night and headed to the car she would call Tobias. Hannah did not want that of course. She knew how important that night was for him and his colleagues.

"Oh Hannah Renee! You are gorgeous." Tearing up Kelly runs for the camera and does a mini photo shoot by the time they leave for the ball.

When Hannah exits the car in front of the five star hotel that required valet parking she does it with a little pizzazz in her step. She pretended not to take notice of the heads that turned as they entered the ballroom that was fit for royalty. Her mind said, "Girl you've still got it and tonight you had better flaunt it." She did just that. Holding her head up high she tried not to remember her husband had tossed her aside for another love. She suddenly knew how her miraculous $5,000 ticket had come to her when she spotted none other than Dr. Gabriel Emmanuel—the schemer who was obviously still single, gorgeous, and full of himself sitting in the seat next to her. His body was still oh so finely sculptured and his smile just as brilliant, but this time he looked older than he should have.

"Hannah, it's good to see you again."

"Likewise" was all she answered.

The room was full of testosterone, ego, and drugs; representatives of course. What a combination Hannah thought to herself. She mostly people watched and tried hard not to excuse herself too often to call and check on her little Joy. The room was elaborately decorated in pink and red; rightly so, and all things designer. Designer bags, suits, shoes, gowns, even designer hair for men and women; some you could take off and ones you could plug in. She just wished for their sakes a fire did not erupt or they were all in trouble.

Tobias and Kelly were genuinely happy and it was observed by all. They found it hard to keep their hands off one another. He just had to touch her hair and she just had to put her hand on his thigh. They smiled and conversed with the other seven guests at the table, but somehow never missed an opportunity to steal a glance at the other or play footsies under the table. Hannah was sorry she'd been reluctant to attend the gala. Most if not all the guests had one thing in common; hope. They either had some family member, co-worker, neighbor, friend, or patient that had been diagnosed with cancer. They celebrated the ones that survived, honored the ones that had fought a good fight, and drove the ones who willingly and tirelessly searched for a cure. She ate very little; her hormones were still a bit sensitive and danced even less. She did honestly try hard to engage in conversation, but it was more work than she thought it would be. When Gabe extended his hand to her she wanted to ignore him, but not wanting to make a spectacle of herself, or disappoint her brother she took it.

"Why Hannah you're a natural at this."

"Thanks."

"Why so quiet this evening? As I remember you never had a problem telling me what was on your mind from our first meeting."

"I'm sorry Gabe, I don't mean to be rude, I'm just a little tired that's all."

"Understandable. How long is your holiday?"

"Next weekend."

"You and I must take a ride in my car before you leave, for old times' sake." His satire makes her laugh, breaking the ice.

"You still have that piece of junk?"

"Now there's the Hannah I know. For your information my car is not junk? It is class you don't understand Lady Hannah."

"Cheap is what I prefer to call it." This time he laughed as he swirled her around then pulled her close again. A few heads looked on in curiosity, Tobias being one of them. He noticed his sister was not wearing the wedding ring that sparkled on her finger upon arrival. Hannah was just enjoying the moment. Their bodies fit well together as they danced first one dance, then another, and another. She couldn't remember the last time she'd danced or felt desirable and both felt good, too good. After the third dance Mrs. Chandler was really tired. She thanked the good doctor and he escorted her back to the table. He pulled out her chair and thanked her for the company on the dance floor. A few minutes later she excused herself and called to tell Joy goodnight. Not quite ready to join the party she found herself admiring the hotel and lost track of time until she heard a voice behind her.

"Hannah…you alright?" Turning she sees Gabe clad in his black tie apparel that was tailored to his body and for a second she wondered what it would be like to…then snapped out of it.

"I'm fine. Thanks for asking, just admiring my surroundings."

"This place is perfect for such an auspicious event isn't it?"

She nodded her head in agreement and the two walk and talk for a minute, then two, then thirty. When her phone chimed to inform her of a message she supposed it was Jane checking on her, but surprisingly it was her brother. The two word message puzzled her, "Be careful." Before she thinks it through, Gabe said something and her attention was drawn to him again and they continued to walk and talk. She learned that they had both loved and lost in the three years since he'd first deceived her. After thinking he'd found the perfect girl he learned that she wasn't ready for a monogamist relationship. Which sent him into seclusion, thus, he had found a cause, and buried himself in his work. According to him he was just emerging from having his head buried in the sand. She'd forgotten just how easy he was to talk to and that he had such a great sense of humor.

Time just slipped away like a drifting ship as they catch up on the happenings of their lives. He was attentive to her every move. If she sat he aided her in doing so. If she paused he waited until she was ready to move on before proceeding. He blessed her when she sneezed, offered water when she coughed, complimented the color in her hair that had been there for weeks and her husband never noticed, and was utterly engrossed in her every word. He ignored his phone while they were together, unlike her husband and was sympathetic about her resent job loss. He even offered to put in a good word for her if she ever decided to relocate to the Tri City area. It felt great to converse with someone who was neutral. Someone that did not force their opinion or advice on her but merely extended an ear. When she fell silent once more, her mind drifting back to her troubles again. He gently touched her on her arm.

"Hey, where have you gone?"

Half smiling she said, "Just day dreaming is all."

"So am I." Something about the way he said it drew Hannah's attention. He was staring at her. Not like he'd ever done before. "Do you know how beautiful you are Hannah? I mean do you really know?"

The atmosphere had changed. Hannah looked at his face in search of that dry humor of his but only desire was present. His eyes were alluring, beckoning her to come to him without reservation. He offered her something she took too long to refuse. When he caressed her she knows she should have discouraged him, but she did not. So he continued, from her hair to her lips ever so softly he ran his fingers across them in a slow provocative gesture. Her heart said no but her mind and her body sang a different tune. What could it hurt she asked herself? It is just harmful flirtation anyway. She knew she was still married and so did he. Maybe she should give Brice a dose of his own medicine. He should have to feel all the pain and rejection that had been inflicted upon her. He deserved to know personally how not good enough felt when it was tattooed on his heart. Maybe she just shouldn't care anymore. She tried to convince herself that girl was not her anymore that needed to be validated. The same little girl that used to want approval and affirmation. The one she thought had changed and moved on to better. That confused little girl she was sure she had buried and thrown flowers on her grave.

When he kissed her the little girl in her cried out, "I just want to be loved that's all. Is that so wrong?" Another part of her said, "This isn't right and you know it. Will you do to him what he has done to you?" She argued with herself, "I should hurt him just like he hurt me" but a voice answered back "But you will only be hurting yourself." He kissed her harder and she became lost in his intoxicating smell, his alluring sexuality, and the need just to be touched and made to feel good again. It felt so good despite the war going on inside her. Why should she respect Brice when he had not respected her? A voice spoke to her again and said, "This is not about Brice, it is about you." His hand moved down her body and hit a spot privy only to her husband and it was like fire. Fire that burned because you knew you weren't supposed to touch it. Fire that burned down to the nerves through the bones and instantly seared your soul. That's when she pulled away feeling indescribable pain, breathing hard, and close to tears.

"I can't Gabe...this isn't right, I'm sorry." Running for her life she located the nearest restroom and burst through its door ignoring the bathroom attendant, she cried bitter tears.

"Miss., are you alright? May I get something for you?" She shook her head no and tried her best to get it together but realized she was trembling so severely it became difficult to remain standing. The attendant, a middle aged Asian woman with the gentlest eyes, did not give up so quickly. "Are you sure I can't get you anything Miss.?"

"I'm sure, thank you Miss."

The attendant extended a cool towel to Hannah and she gratefully accepted it. "Thank you."

"My pleasure."

Having gathered herself as best she could, Hannah proceeded to exit the room but then decided to take the attendant up on her offer to help.

"Miss., can you tell me how I can get a taxi to the Kingdom Villas?"

"Most certainly" the woman answered smiling.

Hannah texted her brother after she was already well on her way home. When she arrived home she offered no explanation for her early return. She scooped up her sleeping little girl and retreated to the guest bedroom; embarrassed, disappointed, and disgusted with herself. She knew God had to feel the same way.

Once she put her daughter to bed she showered and hung the dress in the closet. She knew she would never wear it again. She told God she was sorry and asked for His forgiveness and strength. It wasn't that she desired Gabe in that way, she just wanted to know what it felt like to be desired, to be appreciated, to matter. She'd lost focus with all the attention Gabe showered upon her. He noticed in just one evening things that Brice hadn't noticed in months. She felt his pain too, and his lost and he felt hers and in some sick way they wanted to console each other. She shuddered thinking about what may have happened if she had not heard that voice. She was emotionally wounded and her heart hurt so much it was looking for someone to heal it and she hadn't even realized it. A minute longer and she would have opened the door to him and sex would have only been an afterthought to a soul tie with the wrong person and a past life she never wanted to repeat.

The next morning she woke up extra early to speak to her brother. Talking to him was going to be the hard part. She didn't know if Gabe told him what happened but she knew she owed him an explanation about running out on one of the most important events of his life.

"I'm sorry about last night T." There, she got it out, and then braced herself for what was to come.

For a minute he did not respond but sat starring into his cup of cocoa. "So am I, but not like you think. I'm sorry that some men don't do it God's way and damage His greatest creation of beauty to the point that it no longer has confidence in itself nor the one that created it. Sorry that some guys can't appreciate God's beauty without feeling they need to violate it for their own personal gain instead of respecting it and loving it enough to appreciate it from a distance. Sorry that you still don't know your worth; that you are priceless, that no one can give you value except you."

"I thought I was above that T. I mean I know God has changed me. I just don't understand what happened. Does that mean I am one of the hypocrites I used to mock? Does it mean God won't love me anymore? Am I a horrible person?"

"No, no and no. You have had two relationships and both have dealt you devastating blows. Your life is painful right now so wisdom says that it is not a good idea to put yourself in any compromising positions. You are wounded and that makes you vulnerable. It doesn't mean that you don't love God or He does not love you, it means you must be careful while you are healing. You've been through a lot Hannah and I know it's been rough, but it can and will get better. Believe it or not it could very well happen to anyone. None of us are above short comings or faults, but the way you cover yourself is surrounding yourself with accountability partners. People you can trust to help you when you are weak, talk to you, and stay by your side until you are stronger."

"I can't see my way through this one. I've always had something to drive me, to look forward to. I've always had something to conquer or live towards, but not this time. When I lost my baby I lost that something."

"What about the child you have? Isn't she enough?"

"Of course she is enough, that's not what I meant."

"Tell me what you meant then."

"I only want Joy's life and my life to get better, not worse. I want to add to her life not subtract. A sibling would have been great for her but a father is even better. When I went to school I looked forward to graduation because it meant I would be doing better for myself; then finding you, things like that. Goals and ambitions that would help me when I wanted to give up. What do I have to offer my little girl now besides a broken home? I always wanted better for my baby. How do I start over and how do I look forward to building my life all over again?"

"You're focusing on the wrong thing. Look at what she has now. She is provided for, she is loved, she has a family that adores her and if you allow him Brice still wants to be her father even if he doesn't want to be your husband. The question, is will you allow him to? That is a pain that Joy doesn't have to endure, give her back her father. I know it may hurt you, but if it is Joy's heart you are concerned with then don't stand in the way of her peace and the love she has for the only father she has ever known. That is maturity Hannah. Don't punish her for the pain you want him to feel."

"I guess."

"No, you know it to be true. For the record I still believe he loves you and I know you love him. Don't give up on your marriage Hannah. It is one of the few things worth fighting for and working through the tough times."

"He's in love with someone else, not me."

"Hmmm, I may be wrong, but I have my serious doubts about that one. Too many things just do not add up." With that he gave her a much needed hug and headed to his patients leaving Hannah with much to think about. There were no other people on the earth that she would allow to be as candid with her as Tobias and Jane, but her brother's words were still difficult to digest. She was aware she was punishing Brice, but couldn't stop. Each day she wanted to dial his number and give the phone to their daughter so she could hear her father's voice but was unable to bring herself to carry out the mental plan that worked so well in her head.

The remaining days in Virginia truly were a vacation for Hannah and her daughter. She had lunch with her brother, shopped with her sister-in-law. Kelly's retail therapy was window shopping, but Hannah went because it meant they were together and that was the priceless part of the deal. The children spent time at the park when the weather wasn't so unbearable. They made family events of every little thing. The only person missing was her husband, especially when they took a trip to the capital. Although Joy was still quite young she thought going to White House was something that every American should experience. She and Brice had spoken often of making the trip when she was older, but she figured now was a good a time as any considering the circumstances.

When the day finally came for them to leave it was a tear jerker. She struggled and was a bit squeamish about facing life at home again, which made Joy fastidious and Kelly somber. Tobias had not been able to accompany them to the airport but said his goodbyes before going into the office and followed up with a quick phone call just before they boarded the plane.

"Hannah, you know you're going to be fine right? As difficult as it may be to grasp what I am saying you must hold on to your faith right now. I know few people that have conquered the adversities you have. You are strong, tenacious, beautiful, and a genius at that. Call me if you need me and never ever think you are alone."

She couldn't answer the brother she loved so much. Life didn't seem like it would ever be fine again. When she was around others that had strong faith she believed, but when all alone, she just did not know. She wavered from one day to the other. She was confident one day then drowning in the uncertainty of the unknown on others. What she did know was that she had to begin to rebuild her life again. She needed to decide if she would find an apartment or rent a home. Obtaining gainful employment was high on her list of to dos. Pressing on her mind were telling Connor about his daughter and the episode in the hospital. Palpable were the words spoken to her. No medication, no grief, nor sorrow could explain them away, but she had to tuck them away until she could get her own life together. Miss. Ann must wait.

Chapter 12

Hannah was back at her Mother's for a little more than a month when she decided it was time for her and little Joy to take a road trip. She was taking her daughter to meet her birth father without anyone's approval. She and her mother had argued about it. If she and Brice had been on speaking terms nothing he could have said would have mattered to her either, especially at this point. Jane had all but gotten in her face and threatened to give her an old fashioned beat down, but she did not listen to any of them. It was time her baby met her father and nothing or no one was going to change that. The only thing that had kept her from telling him the truth was Brice. He was no longer a factor now. She did not want her daughter to go through life wondering. She did not want her to have a Miss. Ann experience because adults were liars and schemers who manipulated the paths of their children to suit their own selfish needs. Connor was the father of Summer Anna-Joy Chandler and he deserved to know it. What he did with that information was solely up to him, but he would know the truth? She had been forced to search her heart time and time again to ensure she wanted Connor to know for the right reasons. Her mother thought maybe she just wanted to hurt Brice. She did want him to hurt as she did sometimes, but the truth was, she would never, could never use her child as pone. Putting Joy in a bad situation would only harm her and she would never intentionally do that to her or anyone else. Frustration was all she felt when attempting to explain her reasons to Jane. No one understood, but she had peace and that was all that mattered.

This time when she crossed city after city she did not feel like she was alone in the world as she had the very first time she made the trip to Washington. Besides the reminder strapped securely in the car seat asking a million questions, she had God. He was the main reason she was making this trip. She didn't want any more secrets. No skeletons from the past to rattle the new life she was determined to build for her and her daughter. She just didn't want to run anymore. Looking over her shoulder thinking that someone was going to show up one day and take her baby away. No, she was facing this head on once and for all. Brice's opinion and no one else's mattered. He was no longer a priority in her life. Her heart had already divorced him and now she was moving on. Not to another relationship as she had done in the past, but to the plans God had for her that she was always hearing about in church.

A day in the life of Hannah the weeks leading up to the trip to Washington was probably as dismal as she ever imagined living. Before when things became challenging she still maintained a job, her health the best she could, and her home all while being as close to clinically depressed as possible. When she had driven herself as far as she could she retreated to her bed and that was where she stayed on her days off and weekends. This time she had no place to call home, no employer, and not a soul she felt she could speak to without having to hear Brice's side of the story. This time when she wanted to pull the covers over her head, Joy was hungry, or wanted to go to the park, wanted to play dolls, or her all-time favorite, wanted to speak to her daddy on the phone. Judging was what she felt the people around her were doing. Judging her for keeping Joy away from her father, for not going to church like she should and for staying to herself so much. The truth was, she thought of no other people in the world besides God, Joy and Brice.

It had been different for her with Brice. He was not only her hero and lover, but her best friend. When she had not been able to see eye to eye with him as a spouse, she could always have tea, in his case a strong cup of coffee, with a friend a talk about her problems. That life was a thing of the past. Yet, she thought about it daily. She missed him, she missed church, and she missed the life they had built as a family. So she talked to God about it every day whether she went to church or not. She remembered the good things about Brice and those things kept her from bad mouthing him to others, including their daughter. Those good things kept her from answering Gabe when he texted to check on her. Even the ones that came when she was lonely out of her mind and hurting like crazy she knew she must not respond. Her brother's words always echoed in her mind. "Keep yourself out of compromising positions." Legally she had a husband and despite what he had done to her she knew she was bound by that document to respect him.

About three days into her trip she knew she was headed in the wrong direction. Somewhere between San Antonio, Texas and Albuquerque, New Mexico something else superseded the pain from her broken marriage and miscarriage that weighed so heavily on her heart at times; Miss. Ann. Part of her thought how unfair for God to interject this into her life when she was going through so much. The other part of her didn't know what she was expected to do. What could she do for Miss. Ann? After putting Joy to bed that night the light bulb came on and she made just one phone call.

"Hello and where are you?"

"We are fine Michael and how are you" she answered being facetious.

"Now you know I have been worried sick about you. You are supposed to check in every two hours and you know it, but oh no, I haven't heard from you since…oh yeah, yesterday."

"You're right and I'm wrong, and I'm sorry."

"What, Hannah Renee wrong."

"It happens, better write it down. You may not get to experience this phenomenon again."

"Where are you?" He was serious and upset, not a good duet for him. The recent dishevel of someone he loved so much was wearing at him and he was not doing a good job at camouflaging it. He was still perturbed about the whole Brice thing, disturbed about the miscarriage, and unnerved about Connor knowing the truth.

"We are in New Mexico, Albuquerque to be exact."

"Text me the hotel information."

"Doing it now."

"Good. When are you scheduled to arrive?"

"I'm not."

"Excuse me."

"I'm headed back home tomorrow. I have something more pressing."

"What's going on Renee? What about this whole Connor thing? Are going to tell him about the baby?"

"Yes, but I think it will be better if I called him. Seeing him might not be a good idea."

"Why. Do you still have feelings for him?"

"Absolutely not! I have a husband remember?"

"Is that what he is? Anyway, my uncle had a wife and a mistress for thirty-three years. They decided which days the other should have him and when he died they planned the funeral together and sat next to one another during the service. Marriage means nothing to people these days."

"Well it means something to me. I don't know if I ever loved Connor as much as I was fascinated with him. When he was good my life was a dream, but when he was naughty, well I have the marks to prove it. Brice was my first love and there is nothing I can do to change that as much as I'd like to."

"Since you can't then allow me."

Ignoring his remarks she asked him the dreaded question, "Michael do you think you can get me a contact for Connor?"

"God Renee, I do not want to be involved with this."

"Please Michael. If anyone can I know that person is you. I'm tired of running Michael. I want the truth to be known so I don't have to fear what may or may not happen anymore. Secrets have all but destroyed my life and you know much about that. I just don't want him to be able to show up at my baby's door one day and announce that he is her father. I don't want her to wonder why we lied to her. Why we kept the truth from her. It is not about me, Connor or Brice, this is about Joy. I need the peace of knowing I was brave enough to do the right thing. I just want my past to be my past so I can have a future. Can you understand that?"

"Yes, I understand more than you will ever know."

"Will you help me, please? All I need is a good number and your support. No one else understands."

"You know me and my girls will always have your back." Hannah knew he was referring to him exercising the right to bear arms. Anyone that really knew him was not fooled by his innocent look, genius brain, or his diversity. He was packing at all times, even on the rare occasion that he went to the house of the Lord. "Give me until noon tomorrow."

"Thank you, thank you, thank you!"

"Alright already don't get all sappy on me."

"I love you Michael and there is nothing you can do about it." She was rubbing it in and he hated every moment of it.

He uttered something in one of the many languages he spoke. She was sure it was not something she could not have shared with her mother's ladies' group, and then said, "Talk to you tomorrow" and ended the call.

Chapter 13

All during the night Hannah continually whispered, "Your plans God, your plans for my life." She wanted to read but couldn't focus. She longed to hear it would be alright but not one of her family members or friends believed she was doing the right thing. Jane had said nothing since the day they argued and her mother was in quiet mode. She said she was just being prayerful, but Hannah called it giving her the cold shoulder or ignoring her. She wondered just what prayer had to do with it at all. The only person that understood just a bit was Tobias. Hannah reminded him of their relationship; the fact that they grew up a street apart and had never known one another. She thought how different her life would be if she had never found her brother, so did he and that was what made him tell her if she felt it was right in her heart then she should tell him the truth. By the time Michael called her around nine o'clock the next morning she was exhausted. Partly from worrying, and the other from rehearsing over and over just what she would say to Connor. It had been some time after five in the morning before she eventually drifted off to sleep.

"Hi Renee, I have something for you. Can't promise you it is a good lead, but it was all I could come up with, for now anyway."

"Shoot."

"One of our old coworkers last contacted him using this number." She was silent for second, almost dismal. The moment of truth was present and she was having cold feet. "Renee."

"I'm here, let me grab a pen, hold on a second." Walking over to the table to grab the pad and pen placed thoughtfully next to the phone she prayed again, "Lord please protect me and my baby. I just want to do what's right. Let your angels be with us please. When she walked back to the bed where she'd left her phone she felt a bit stronger. "Okay Michael, I'm ready." As she jotted the number down she had an assurance in her heart that she was making the correct decision.

"Thanks Michael."

"No problem at all. Are you alright this morning? You seem a bit distant and I know you are only that way when you have things on your mind."

"Oh no. I'm just peachy. I really really appreciate this, thanks."

"You know I will go to the end of the earth for you now don't you?"

"Yes, I do and I can't tell you what that means to me to know I have someone in my corner no matter what."

"That's what friends do."

"One day I'm going to be that kind of friend to you Michael. One day you won't always have to listen to my problems and rescue me and fight my battles because I will be fine."

"You are a fighter. I would rather be on your team than anyone else's in the world Renee, I love you."

"I love you too. You are the one person I can depend on all the time." She didn't know, had never known he had always loved her from the very beginning. Connor did, and that was why he hated him so much. He thought it best to keep that between him and God because he did not think she could handle one more thing. "I will call you after I speak to him."

"You had better or I will be on a plane headed to Texas." He was serious and she knew it.

It was a tedious drive home. Texas had been hit with a stream of storms and Hannah and Joy were caught in the middle of them. She had nowhere to turn, being in the middle of nowhere. Having too far to go back she drove forward through the rain, lightening, and hail; praying like she had never prayed before. She wasn't afraid. She prayed for guidance for her daughter, her marriage, and for how to execute whatever it was God wanted her to do for Miss. Ann. She also asked that she recognize the correct timing to call Connor. Two days had come and gone and she held on to the number still. Maybe she wanted to be closer to home before making the call. She didn't know but in the meantime she continued to make her way back to San Antonio until she was in her mother's driveway.

When they walked into the house Joy ran straight into her grandmother's arms and so did she. They both cried. Their words had been bitter before her trip and that was not like her mother. That was Hannah, at least the old Hannah and every now and then the God is still working on me Hannah, the sometimes I just have to get you off my back Hannah, so if you push me I will shove you back Hannah. "Forgive me Mommy. I said some things and I shouldn't have."

"So did I and I ask you to please forgive me."

It wasn't until Joy said, "Ouch" that the two realized they are squeezing Joy who had been caught in the middle of them. Joy immediately demanded all of her grandmother's attention and that is just what Hannah needed to unpack the car and shower. Having been riding in the car for days Joy was now running around the house like a wild child and there was nothing either of them could do to detain her.

"Joy would you like for Grammy to take you to the jumping store?" Her scream was all the answer her grandmother needed. Hannah did not feel much like getting back into a car so soon but she knew it was what all of them needed. Her mother had not asked her any details about the trip but she planned to tell her everything the first chance she was given. She already had to know something was up because they returned earlier than expected.

Watching her little girl jump and jump and jump was amazing. Her smile was as big as her heart. She looked like Connor but her mannerism was all Brice. A part of her was longing to converse with him again, as tragic as it sounded to even her own mind. She wondered how Italy had been for him and if he was really sorry for what he'd done or if he was just saying what she wanted to hear. It had been five months. Five long painful, cry yourself to sleep, I wish we were better, I still can't find employment, I miss my friend, I'm a bad person because I know you love your daughter and she needs you, I don't always go to church, how can I still love you months.

After they were both sure Joy had exerted all of her energy they packed her up and went to the Hot Dog Shack, Joy's favorite food place, then headed home. Before they pulled onto the interstate the Joy of both their lives was fast asleep. Hannah smiled at her baby; she was such a beautiful child. What made her snap a mobile picture of her and send it to Brice she will never know, but she did. His response was immediate, "This made my day, thank you." She did not respond.

When Joy was put to bed and the only sounds in the house were the low muffled sounds coming from her mother's television she walked down to her room and lightly knocked on the opened door. When she beckoned for her to come in Hannah walked in and sat on the foot of the bed. "Are you busy Mommy?"

"Never too busy for you Baby Girl" she said putting away the book she was reading.

"I didn't tell him Mommy. Half way through the trip I realized that I shouldn't talk to him in person."

"Why?" a curious Johanna wanted to know.

"Something happened when I was in the hospital Mommy and I knew I needed to get back and take care of it. I think God wants me to do something."

"Do what? I thought you felt Connor needed to know about Joy."

"He does, but maybe I wasn't supposed to go out there, just call him."

With raised eyebrows the concerned mother inquired further. "Have you spoken to him?"

"Not yet, but I plan to. I have a contact but I just did not want to be so far away when I spoke to him. I needed a safe place so I came home. Does that sound crazy?"

Smiling she replied, "Not at all." Her heart warmed knowing her daughter knew she could always come home despite the friction between them.

"Mommy do you know how it feels to not know who you are or where you came from?"

"No Baby Girl, I can't say that I do."

"Exactly, you've always had that confidence because you know your past so you can embrace your future. I don't want my daughter to grow up living a lie, I want to tell her who she is and where she came from because that is my job as a mother. The Bible says we are supposed to be honest and this is where I must start, for her sake and mine. When I slept with

Connor I put myself in this position and so I have to be honest enough and woman enough to stop running, hiding and lying. He is her father and that is that. Do I want him to be a part of our lives? No, not at all, but I remember what it felt like growing up without a father. I remember when my mother died how it felt thinking I had no one in this world only to find out that my birth mother had been raising me, if you can call it that, all along. God forbid I put her in a compromising situation because of my decision, but she will never have to go looking for the truth because I won't keep it from her. That is just respect, something I wish the adults in my life had given me just a little of. I won't tell you it is not scary, but I do know I ended my relationship with Connor all wrong, I left the wrong way, and if I am to ever have the life I dream of whether married or single, I have to face my past. This is something that I must do. I know you don't understand it or agree with it, but Mommy in my heart I know it is the right thing to do. I just need your support. You said God put us together and I believe that with all my heart, but did God mean only when you agree with my actions? You and I both know I am going to make some mistakes, but I still need you Mommy. Please don't stop loving me like everyone else has."

"Oh baby, I will never stop loving you. My heart hurts that I give you that impression." She opened her arms wide and beckoned for Hannah to come closer to her. Her eyes were moist with tears as a result of seeing the pain in her daughter's eyes. The daughter she believed God to give her for so many years. The one she prayed for year after year until one day Renee Corel-Waiters came waltzing into Terrofare International and at first sight she knew her child had finally come.

"I love you Mommy. I don't always know how to do things like I should. Just know I am doing my best, mistakes and all."

Her mother had Hannah's head in her lap and she rubbed her head and prayed. Hannah was not aware of the prayer part, but she did feel peace returning to her that she questioned if she would ever feel again. She was tired; physical, mentally, and spiritually. She had no idea if she was getting the God thing correctly. Most days she was certain she was failing at that as well. The difference, unlike times before, was that she was not going to stop trying. If she fell one hundred times she had made up her mind to get up one hundred and one times. Just before she drifted off to sleep lying across her mother's bed she heard her mother softly humming, "Yes, Jesus loves me." Her own mother had sung that song to her up until the day she was killed in the automobile accident. Something about her God given mother singing it was as if heaven was agreeing with what she was about to do.

Early the following morning while her mother was in her prayer room and Joy still slept Hannah dialed the number. The answer was immediate.

Immediately recognizing her voice, the still half asleep groggy voice said, "Renee…"

"Yes Connor, it's me." Neither of them remembered it was 4:30a.m. in his world and 6:30a.m. in hers. She just prayed to get through the conversation without starting a war. She knew he would be angry; he had every right to be. Hadn't she done to him what her family had done to her? She just did not want to fight about it.

"What's going on Renee? Are you well?"

"Yes Connor, I'm well. I need to talk to you, to tell you something."

"Oh boy, this can't be good Renee. You've been gone for so long and now you call like this."

"I know I left wrong and I apologize for not remembering the time difference. Do you want me to call you back in a little while?"

"**** no! Talk to me, I think you owe me that much."

"You're right, I do." Taking a deep breathe she tried to figure out where to begin, but he interrupted with, "Why Renee, why did you leave me?"

"We weren't right for each other Connor. Deep down inside I believe you knew that. I think we were just rehab for one another. You were running from your father and I was on the run from Brice and life itself."

"No, you ran, I stayed here waiting for you to come home so I could make things right. I'm not my father and I will never be like him. Why couldn't you keep trying Love? Wasn't I worth it, weren't we worth it?"

"Connor that was a long time ago."

"You called me Renee, what is it that you expected?"

"I've moved on Connor, I got married…"

"What!" He goes off into a tantrum filled with obscenities. Hannah moved the phone away from her ear and looked up to heaven for some help. When he was finally finished they were both silent until he must have thought about the situation again and the words just flew out of his mouth once more, no holds barred until she said, "You have a daughter Connor." Then he was speechless. She used the sudden silence as an opportunity to tell him what she should have told him two years earlier. "That day we fought about your father, the day we broke up I was pregnant, but I didn't know it. When I concluded you and I were a thing of the past, or so it seemed. I was scared, I didn't know where to go, the doctor said I needed to rest. That's when I went to Jane's. I never intended to stay but the pregnancy became very complicated and the baby's life was in jeopardy so I had no other choice but to stay out here."

"Who did you marry Renee?"

"Excuse me…"

"Who…did… you… marry?" Each word was laced with bitterness.

"Brice Chandler."

"I don't believe this crap! You left me for him and now he's raising my child! You are a cold witch and I don't know what I ever saw in you."

"Don't you want to know about your daughter Connor? She is not the typical two year old. She's beautiful, she witty, she's smart and she looks just like you. She has your hair, your eyes…" He interrupted her, "Why Renee? Why couldn't we work it out? Why couldn't we raise our daughter together, be a family. God Renee, I love you so much, why did you do this?"

"Aren't you forgetting something Connor? Your racist father ring any bells? Your entire family that hate people of color, or how did they put it, "The ignorant and lazy of our society." I never wanted her to be mistreated Connor. Don't you remember how he made you feel that night? I saw the pain all over your face. He was so demeaning towards you, so belittling, you didn't deserve that and neither does she. You should have a picture of her now. Open it up when you are ready, I have to go."

"No, wait, do you love him Renee? Is he good to you and our baby?"

"You know what I went through as a child so you know I would never allow anyone to mistreat my baby, no one. He loves her and he is great with her and to her. They are two peas in a pod. Now I really have to go."

"You didn't completely answer the question Renee. Do you love him?"

"Yes Connor, I love him."

"Is he good to you? That's all I want to know and I swear I will hang up. Is he good to you?"

The pause told him all he needed to know. She was trying to think of exactly what to say without putting him in their business, but drew a blank for a moment then tried to make a comeback with, "He's a great provider and father. He takes great care of us. If you ever want to talk about our daughter this is my number; otherwise, be good Connor."

With that she hung up the phone and put her face in her pillow. Old habits were so hard to break. She would bet her life on it that if she picked up the phone and told Connor she wanted to come home he would have been on the next flight out willing to try again, but she knew he wasn't right for her. She knew he was toxic for her. She knew he would be everything she needed for a while, and then the honeymoon would end, and the fighting begin. He was a fixer and she was a runner and neither were great relationship material. She wanted, needed somebody, but she knew it couldn't be Connor.

Crying her eyes out in her pillow so her baby could not hear her she tried to forget all the good times they did have together. He was there when work was grueling, when she found her brother and right by her side when Tobias was in the hospital. He taught her how to invest her money and to manage it. He introduced her to a world that she never would have been privy to and had given her the greatest gift in the world in their daughter. She hated to admit it but there never really had been any closure with Connor, Jane was right about that one. He was her first long term relationship. He had rescued her just like Brice had and now just like she walked away from Connor without trying to make it work, she was walking away from Brice.

After her mother's death, before Brice, and before Connor she'd never had anyone to console her, to hold her, or to kiss her boo boos and make them better. Never once was there a high five or good job, not one person at her honors day programs, or her awards ceremonies. Then Jane came along and her family and Brice, but she was too afraid and could allow them to only see so much of her, touch only parts of her soul. By the time Connor came along she just wanted love and it didn't matter the cost. It had cost her much in the end but she had been willing to pay the price until God started whispering things in her ear. A part of her knew if she allowed herself she could run back and forth to Connor for the rest of her life. She knew she had to close the door forever. What part of her she had lost in their relationship God would have to heal.

Still on her knees severely broken, hurt, and feeling alone she heard God speak to her heart again, "I'm here." She was surprised to hear her own voice say, "Lord I want my marriage to work. I want my husband back, I want my family." It was the same prayer her husband had been praying for months. She never saw her mother in the shadows of the hall crying for her baby and asking God to mend her heart. It was the most difficult thing in the world to step aside and watch your children grow up.

Chapter 14

One morning Hannah wakes to the sound of a light rain pelting the windows, and a soft wind dancing through the rose bushes in the back yard and little Joy having a conversation on her toy phone.

"Hi Daddy. I miss you to the moon and back. Daddy please come and get me, I want to play." After completing her pretend conversation she gives her doll Dixie a turn. "Daddy say Hi to Dixie. Dixie talk to Daddy." When Dixie speaks in Joy's voice of course she says, "I sorry, I sorry for being a bad girl. I be a good girl so I can have story time and go to the park, okay Daddy? Okay, I be a real good girl for you to come see me."

It was just too much for Hannah. Seeing what she had willingly done to her daughter pierced her heart. Unlike Connor, he was willing and ready to be a father in every capacity. The problems between her and her husband were not and should have never been between Joy and him. Joy loved him and no space or time between them was ever going to change that. After showering and making breakfast she stepped out into the cool autumn air and made a phone call. The phone rang continually and then the voice recording played. She hung up deciding against leaving a message. By the time she slide the glass door open to return to the house her phone was ringing.

"Hi Brice."

"Hi Han." She thought she was ready to hear his voice and that she could handle it but there had been a miscommunication between her brain and her heart. "I was returning your call. I don't know if it was an accident or not, but I couldn't take the chance." His tone was hopeful yet cautious.

"No, it wasn't an accident. Joy wants to talk to you."

"Really? Excited he asked, "Where is my little princess?"

"She's inside. Maybe you could take her to a movie or something, I mean, if you want to."

"There is nothing in this world I would like more than to spend some time with my baby Han. God I miss her so much, I miss us Han."

"Please Brice, I can't right now."

"Thanks for my picture." She felt the conversation veering in a direction she was emotionally unprepared to venture into.

"You are welcome. What time do you want me to have her ready Brice?"

"What if I took her for ice cream when I get off work and tomorrow we can do a matinee? I mean if you're fine with it and all."

"What time?"

"I will be there at 5 o'clock sharp, traffic being cooperative."

"She'll be ready."

"Thanks Hannah, this means the world to me."

"Brice I have to go. She'll be ready, good-bye."

Doing the right thing was not easy. Sometimes it hurt like the hell she was trying to avoid spending eternity in. Maybe they should give a special class when you sign up for the do right journey. Someone should let the new comers know that life does not suddenly become easy. All of your problems do not disappear and healing was still going to be a process. Everything was not suddenly new like they sang so often in Jane's family church. You have to deal with the same old stuff you had before you said I do to God. He just helped you do it and He helped you through it. Hannah knew that first hand because only God alone was helping her in the seconds, minutes, hours, of her day to day living.

When Brice arrived at 5:15 the next afternoon overly apologetic about the rush hour traffic she did not make eye contact with him. She could not allow him to see her, not that afternoon, not ever again. Joy was bouncing off the walls once she saw him standing over her as she sat at her desk coloring. "Daddy, daddy, daddy, oh daddy, I so missed you daddy" she managed to get out before the tears came. Brice was no good after that. He had always been and she suspected would always be a sucker for Joy. He held her tightly pretending he had something in his eye when she reached up to wipe his tears away.

"Go give Mommy a hug and a kiss so we can go get ice cream." Brice was smiling and somehow it made her feel like she had done something right for a change. Joy's hug and quick, "Love you to en fen da tee Mommy!" was another clue that she was doing the right thing. Even if it did mean she was going to be at home on a Friday night alone. Even her mother had a date yet she was married and still did not have a man.

"What time do I have to bring her back?" Seeing daddy and daughter standing hand in hand somehow gave Hannah hope.

"Tomorrow's Saturday so it's your call Brice." Even her husband was shocked at her reply. The way he snapped his neck around to make sure he was hearing right was one indicator. The other was the quick peck on the check he gave his wife and the boyish grin he wore until they were out of sight.

Hannah Renee was all alone, at least for a few hours anyway. What on earth was there to do? The house was clean already, her and Joy's laundry was completed, her unemployment had been filed and at present she was drowning in sheer boredom. After surfing the net and flipping through the many television channels she retrieved her phone and called her best friend and sister whom she could not stay angry with because it just wasn't possible.

"What took you so long Miss. Thang?"

"Now see that is just like a Cajun. You must have the last word, now don't you?"

"Got that right, now start talking because I know you have a lot to say."

"Not as much as you would like me to that's for sure."

"Well, did you see Connor?"

"Nope. Didn't see him at all."

"What! You really know how to suck all the juice out of gossip don't you?"

"This is my life you are talking about here."

"Spicy as it may be, I still wanted to hear about that red head you used to shack up with. I've seen his pictures, that man is fine. Sorry but he says eleven on my radar all day long."

"See, you are so nasty. What happened to Mr. Parking lot attendant?"

"Oh Chile, he still has me attending services on a regular basis. Pretty soon they are going to mistake me for a member."

"And you say my life has drama?"

"Well I didn't say you were the only one with issues. It is just better to talk about other people's that's all. You know that. Where is my niece anyway? It is too early for her to be in bed and too quiet for her to be awake."

"With her daddy."

"What! Her daddy? What daddy? Girl you had better start talking." The octaves of Jane's voice were escalating by the second. Hannah always knew she was dramatic, but that day it was on overdrive.

"You should stop by, better yet why don't we go to the theater? It has been a moment since I have done anything but cry my eyes out. I think it's time I rediscovered the world. Plus I must confess. I didn't tell you that the good doctor had his tongue in my mouth."

After the screams subside she said, "I will be there in fifteen minutes, twenty if the cops are out."

"Please stop speeding because public transportation can't handle you. I would hate to have to see a viral video of you beating up some poor passenger or transit driver."

"Whatever, just be ready Missy, I'm already in my car."

True to her word Jane was coming down her mother's driveway in exactly fifteen minutes. It was good to see her friend, heck it was great to get out of the house and even better to have a small break from life for a minute. Scared of allowing Joy out of her sight the last several weeks and then months had been so stressful. She didn't want to lose anything else. Her job was no more, her marriage was about to end in divorce, and the baby was gone. To top that off all of her relationships had been tested to include her mother's and Jane's. She just did not know where to turn. God should have been the obvious answer but sadly He wasn't in too many instances. The only thing she did was apply for jobs, go to doctor's appointments, take care of her daughter, and help out around the house when allowed. If someone had taken her to the future and showed her this life she was living she would have disputed it fervently. How could a grown woman, married at that, be highly educated, be unemployed and living at home with her mother? Her life as she saw it was a train wreck, but she was about to resolve all that.

"Hey Jennifer."

"So it's like that aye?"

"I missed you Jane." Hannah just had to get it out. "I really really missed you."

"I missed you too Han."

"So why did I have to be the first to call?"

"I just figured you needed your space. I knew when you were ready you would come around."

"What if I never got ready Jane? Would our friendship have dissolved?"

"Heyyy, where is all this coming from? You know hell would have to freeze over before you and I parted ways. What's wrong, talk to me? Your mood is scaring me and you know it takes a lot to scare me."

"Nothing. Where is my little man?"

"With my aunt and that is the biggest nothing I have ever had the pleasure of meeting. I know I was curt with you about Connor Han but I just don't want to see you or my goddaughter hurt. I was scared so I spoke out of my fear. Especially when you told me about those crazy dreams that lady at your church had about you. I mean that was some creepy stuff and you know it. I'm still in your corner."

"I'm doing the best I can with what I have and what I know. Anyway, I told Connor."

"What did he say?"

"Not a whole lot actually. He was more concerned about me and who I married and why I left."

"What was your reply?"

"I told him. I owed him that much."

"Negative. You owe him nothing."

"He deserved to know the truth about his daughter. If he had known about the pregnancy and still chose not to know his child that would have been different. I never gave him that option."

"So now what?"

"We wait. He hasn't contacted me since our conversation, but I know I did the right thing by him and that is enough for me."

"So Joy is with Brice then?"

"Yes."

"Since when?"

"Since I called him and he picked her up after work this afternoon. He's also taking her to the theater tomorrow."

"Wow, that's a drastic change and so sudden. To what might I contribute it to?"

They talked about the doll incident and the guilt Hannah was having for keeping Joy away from her daddy. They talked about the fact that Hannah felt like a whore because she kissed or at least allowed another man to kiss her and fondle her inappropriately. They talked and talked and talked, just to talk.

"Han let me tell you something, I know a whore when I see one and believe me, you my dear are not it. A whore would be that trick name Shiloh in the apartments at my cousin's building who was doing the daddy and the son. Now that is a whore. How about this girl name Mixie I knew in high school who took care of the whole football team. When she got pregnant all of them were afraid, to include the coach. She didn't even bother to have a DNA test done, she just called the child huddle and no one had to ask why. Let's not forget Kenny from college. I know you remember him. They knew that boy on a first name basic down at the health clinic. Honey the nurses and the doctors nick named him, "Got something" because every time he came in to see them he had something; herpes, VD, and some other things I can't pronounce but I know he had it. Girl every time he came through the food court line we threw out his silverware. We never bothered to send it through the dishwasher because we knew he had something. For him it didn't matter who it was he or she, he just wanted it. You Han who has only slept with two men in your natural born life, one being the man you married, do not fit the criteria baby cakes."

"Now see there you go, can't ever be serious. You and your stories."

"Chile, those are no stories, I can write a book about whoreolgy. I think I may call it, "Wham, Bam, no thank you Ma'am, I don't want none of that! I have had one or two myself. You remember my ex-boyfriend who was always tired, always broke, and always taking care of his sick mother.

Yeah, he was tired because he was doing me, Keyera and Sofia. Turns out his mother was dead, but he did have an active prescription for that can make you have an erection for up to four hours medication. Well, let's just say he made full use of all four of those hours. I still have myself tested for HIV, PID, and anything else new they come up with. He was the one that helped me get my degree in sex gone wrong university."

Hannah had to laugh despite trying to be serious. Jane was totally serious and that made it even funnier.

"So why do you think the good doctor crossed the line anyway. He didn't strike me as that type of person when you described him to me."

"Who knows? He had a bad break up; I was in a bad situation and the rest I can't tell you."

"Do you think he would have gone all the way if you hadn't stopped him?"

"Yes, No, Maybe, oh who can tell. I'm just glad it didn't. I can't lie, the first time I met him I was attracted to him, but it was just sex appeal like someone you see on television or something. But, I wasn't married then and it was just innocent. Plus, that was all so long ago. I wasn't thinking of him that way at all that day. Maybe that was a part of why I can give Brice a little leeway. My conscience could not handle going any further with Gabe, but maybe Brice doesn't have one."

"Yeah right. We all have a conscience. As much of a heathen as I am sometimes I still know right from wrong. Although sometimes it is not that simply though. You can get yourself into situations you think it will be easy to walk out of sometimes only to discover you are trapped. What's easy to get into most times is not as easy to walk out of, believe me." Jane was thinking of the church boy who was trying to do right but could not leave her alone. Every time they slept together she was scared that lightening was going to strike them both. They tried to have only phone conversations or casual acquaintance but always ended up sleeping together. When she saw him at one end of the altar every now and then it almost broke her heart because she was certain she was coming between him and God, but they could not stop. She broke it off out of guilt and fear, but he came by just to say Hi and sex it was. She got lonely at night and a simply text turned into sex once again. She attempted to talk to one of the ladies on her job that she thought had some clout with God, but she told her if it was meant to be, then it was not wrong. She wasn't an expert on God but she knew it was something tragic about her advice and never went back again. When Hannah interrupted Jane's thoughts she was relieved.

"Jane why do I still love Brice so much? Is it because I'm afraid to fail again? Or if I'm trying to prove everybody wrong about us? I know we married quickly and we or I at least had a lot going on when we got back together. I just don't understand. The minute I gave myself permission to love without reservation my life fell apart."

Jane, who was always full of advice now had none. They both had questions that did not seem to have answers. The rest of the evening was spent idly watching a movie neither of them enjoyed and eating food either of them savored. Life was on their mind and it weighed heavily.

Chapter 15

When Brice returned with a super hyper, had too much junk food Joy, Hannah was sitting at the desk in her mother's study. He stood around seemingly needing to say something that was never uttered. She pretended to be engrossed in the computer and tried to act like she did not notice. For a while they sat; he on the plush black loveseat and her on the swivel back office chair. Joy was playing with some new toy he had purchased for her and was content for the moment. They did not know what to do with themselves. Months had passed since the couple that was inseparable and so in love had spent so much time in one another's presence. He noticed her weight lost and the tired look on her face. He noticed the bags under her beautiful eyes and the new hair color that made them twinkle. He saw the way she constantly twirled her hair or nibbled at her bottom lip periodically and knew she was not content or happy. When she was happy the dimple in her cheek was as deep as the sea when she made any kind of facial expression. When she was happy you wouldn't catch her on a computer to save her soul because that was what she did at work and never at home. When she was happy she lite-up when he came into the room and showered him with hugs and kisses. He wanted to make her happy again, but had the sinking feeling that maybe he would never be able to. All he ever wanted to do was be Hannah's man and give her the world. Thinking about it now he realized that was crazy. How could he give her something that never belonged to him? Suddenly she turned from her position on the computer and he did not like what she had to say.

"Brice, will you sign the divorce papers, please. You always said you only wanted what was best for us. Maybe this is best."

"For who Hannah? Can't we go to counseling?"

"You may. I just want out Brice. Please just do this last thing for me."

He told himself he wanted to make her happy and maybe this was his only chance so he said, "Give me this weekend with my daughter please. Allow her to spend Saturday night with me, at home after we go to the theater and whatever else we decide to do. I'd like to take her to the park on Sunday after church and out to dinner please. If you will give me just this weekend with my baby then you can bring the papers to the house on Monday after I get off work and I will sign them. My desire is to see you happy. I don't want to cause you anymore pain. I know this is all my fault and I also know I can't make you forgive me."

"Does she have to spend the night Brice? I've never been without my baby overnight since she came into the world."

"I wish I could say that. I could until the day you left." He spaced out for a moment and then asked, "Do you think I would hurt her Han?"

He looked at her with such pain in his eyes it was difficult for her to look back at him, but she does, for longer than she should have. She heard a voice whisper, "Forgive him, just forgive him so both of you can be happy again. So you can have your family back. I'll make it better than before if you trust me." She ignored it.

"No Brice, I know you would never hurt her. If I know nothing else I know you love Summer Anna-Joy Chandler." His eyes pierced through her soul and she does not, cannot break the magnetic trance that had imprisoned them both. He wanted forgiveness, she wanted love. He wanted his wife, she needed her husband. He wanted another chance, she wanted to take a chance. When he stepped towards her she held her breath and waited, but just before he reached his wife little Joy began to jump up and down demanding that he take her outside to ride her car. The moment passed and they both embraced regret as he headed outside and she to her bedroom.

For the remainder of the time he was at the house he engrossed himself with his daughter. From the window Hannah watched them when they weren't paying attention. He was two people; part happy, part sad. Joy knew something was going on and pushed him to the limit about getting her way whenever possible. "Daddy may I have ice cream before bed? I want to play ball in the house. May I stay up late? No I want to watch that show Daddy!" He was just happy to be with her and she with him, but when his little girl wasn't looking his continence fell and his shoulders slouched.

Brice gave Joy her bath, read her a bedtime story, and tucked her in bed just as he would have had they been at 7289 Callahan Drive. The only difference was he couldn't shower and lay next to his wife once his daughter fell asleep. This time when he left he made no attempt to kiss her. He said a soft good-bye and that was that until he would return at noon the following day to take his daughter home for one last night. His heart ached and his mind was boggled as he drove home alone. For a while he sat in the garage not wanting to face the silence or the pain. He had made a mistake and that night he didn't think he would ever be able to live past it, gain his family's love, trust, or respect again. Hannah and Joy on the other hand were a different story. When her mother came home from her date with the women at the shelter for battered and abused, the two were fast asleep. Joy was plain worn out from daddy time, but Hannah had used a little help from the medicine cabinet. That night her pain was just too great to handle alone.

The next morning she spent extra time with Joy. She made her special panny cakes as she called them, they played dress up, and a game of hide and seek before the time came. She took her time doing her hair the way Brice preferred it and dressed her like a little girl as he always insisted. Her bag was packed and her favorite toy in hand when he rang the doorbell at precisely twelve o'clock. The communication between the two was a minimum; only a need to know basic as related to their daughter. The new allergy medication she was recently prescribed that must be administered in the mornings. The special cream to be used as needed for the eczema and the recent discovery that she was allergic to a particular brand of washing detergent. Joy kissed her Mommy, her Grammy and Brice said his goodbyes to them both and he and his daughter were gone.

When the door closed, her mother wanted to know. "Are you going to be alright Baby Girl?"

Hannah was in shut down mode again and did not feel much like talking, but she would not be rude. The truth was she did not know the answer to her mother's question. Never had she gone through a divorce before. Never had she allowed her daughter to sleep over night with anyone. How would she know if she was going to be alright, but she said, "Yes Ma'am, I will be just fine."

"Yes, you will; no matter what it looks like." This she said and walked away. Hannah breathed a sigh of relieve, but it was short lived when her mother reappeared. "Baby Girl, you have to give herself permission to love your husband publicly. I know you love him and want to forgive him. Don't be concerned about what anyone else thinks about your decisions and don't think you have to handle your marriage or his infidelity the way others have handled theirs. He gave you a chance after you left and when you came home with another man's child he did not turn his back on you, but welcomed you with open arms. He loved you when you were a mess because he believed in you. Up until this happened tell me where was the fault in him? When did he not provide for you and Joy? When did he not love you or her? When did he not come home? Did he tell you how to dress, you had to work, cook, or anything else except be you? Was there ever a time?"

"No Ma'am."

"Then I say go home. Not because I don't love having you and my granddaughter around, but because that is where you belong, together. If you can honestly say you know without any doubt it is over, that it is not worth saving, and quitting is the best thing, then I will support you in whatever you do."

"Mommy I don't mean to sound disrespectful, but that is all easier said than done. It is easy to say when you haven't been through it."

"See that is where you are wrong. I have walked this walk so I am well able to talk this talk."

"How? Your husband loved you until the day he died. You had a great marriage, you told me so yourself."

"Yes he did and we did, but sometimes it takes trouble to make you appreciate what you have. My marriage wasn't without trouble. It did not come great, it was made great one decision at a time. He cheated during our second year together and I wanted out and so did he. We both wanted out because we just knew that was best for us. We put the house on the market and I packed up my things and he so generously offered to drive me back to Mother's house. Something happened on the way there. We were in an accident and the truck we were in went over an embankment and we were both severely injured. He lay bleeding and I was trapped in the vehicle. We yelled, screamed, and cried to finally conclude that no one was coming to rescue us. A day went by and then two and we lay there burning up during the day and freezing at night. By the third day we realized that we might not make it out alive and begin to talk, really talk. There is something about having what you think is your last conversation. We talked about our first date, the way we met. We started to remember just why we married in the first place. We remembered the promises we made to each other. When we thought we were going to die we were happy we were together. That was the only place we would want to be, in each other's arms. So he told me he loved me and apologized for breaking my heart. I forgave him and told him I would always love him and we closed our eyes and prepared to die. The next morning we woke to bright lights shining in our faces. Hunters had discovered our vehicle that had not been visible from the part of the road where we went off. That accident taught us how to live."

"How is that possible?"

"We learned from that near tragedy to live each day as if you were dying. Choose the words you would want that person to hear and remember you by, no others. Choose the people you want to express your love to in those final hours and pour out yourself to them, no excuses. That was the way we lived for the next twenty-five years. Asking ourselves one simply question, "Is that how you want to be remembered?" If you answer no, then don't do it. If yes, then do it with all of your heart, no regrets. It will teach you to forgive quickly and love harder."

Hannah couldn't believe her ears. Johanna had not bothered to share that particular detail of her life and it had her feeling worse off than she had ever been. She just did not know what to think or do. When her mother begun speaking again she had her undivided attention.

"Let me ask you a question Hannah. If you knew that tomorrow was your last day on earth where would you want to be, here with me or home with your husband?"

Hannah doesn't have the strength to answer and her mother knows the answer already so she was not alarmed or offended when she got up and went to her daughter's bed for the night. When the phone rang later that night she eagerly picked it up and said goodnight to her little princess. She was saddened when her husband hung up the phone without saying a word when Joy became tired of talking. She was so torn. She desperately tried to figure out what was real and what was just her emotions toying with her. What if she went back and it just did not work. What if Brice was just guilty or he only stayed because of their daughter? What if he went back to his mistress? What would she do? How many times were you supposed to forgive a cheating man? How much was enough? She still had no answers. Tired but unable to fall asleep she again went to the medicine cabinet around three in the morning.

Her mother did not disturb her when she left the house for church. She did not need to guess that her daughter would not be attending services again that Sunday morning. It had become a habit for her but Johanna did not feel she needed to push God on her as much as she needed to give her the love she needed so dreadfully. They were one in the same, God and love, so she just decided to love her through her difficult time. She was sure it was a worthy investment.

When Brice returned their daughter late that Sunday evening his wife had not done much that day besides pray. She wasn't hungry, she didn't find television interested and she could not concentrate on reading, so she just lay around the house after cleaning it twice. Her mother had already prepared dinner the night before so there was nothing else she could throw herself into besides the bed. After hugging Joy for the third time he looked up at his wife and said, "See you tomorrow Hannah?"

She was thrown by the fact that he used her former name. Throughout college, their brief dating experience and their marriage she had been Han to him. The pet name he came up with and everyone else copied. If he said anything else besides Han he was upset with her, extremely upset. When he called out her name during their love making, it was Han. When he checked on her during the day, it was Han. Even when she irritated him, it was still Han. She guessed that was the answer she had been seeking. He had given up too. She knew it was over because now no one was fighting for them. She said a quick, "Sure, see you tomorrow" and closed the door.

That night she did not sleep at all. She lay awake staring at the walls at times and looking at the stars through the small opening of the curtain. She did not understand why she felt sad knowing it was over. It was what she had asked for, begged for, and prayed for so why was she acting in such a manner? About five in the morning she rolled out of bed and went to her mother's prayer room for two reasons; she knew she would find her there and she knew God was sure to be there too. She needed God.

Her Mother wasn't surprised to see her, or if she was she didn't display it. She went about her regular routine and allowed her daughter to create her own. They both poured out their hearts and before long Johanna was sobbing deep in prayer. Hannah had never heard anyone pray that way before; she told God everything. Hannah said a lot of silent prayers and asked for forgiveness repeatedly. After being honest with God as much as she knew she fell asleep there on the carpet and slept until she heard her baby crying out for her around eight in the morning. By the time she arrived to the bedroom her mother was already there consoling her and promising to make panny cakes special just for her. She encouraged Hannah to get some rest because she knew she had not slept the night before. Hannah didn't want to but her body said if you do not you will pay for it, so she kissed her baby and went to bed.

This time she did sleep. She slept so hard she dreamed that she was running for her life once again. Sometimes she was crying and other times she was fighting. At times Johanna helped her and sometimes Jane, but when things became really really tough, it was Brice that held her hand. That puzzled her. He was taller than he actually was in reality, much taller. He had such large hands and his mouth was abnormal. It was shaped like a dagger or some type of weapon every time he spoke whatever she was running from stood frozen. She on the other hand willingly went with him sometimes and in other instances he had to drag her kicking and screaming. Many times she just gave up and then he would encourage her and she found the strength to get up again. When she awakened it was because her own voice roused her. The words, "Thy Kingdom come, thy will be done" echoed in the room.

Chapter 16

When she pulled into the place that she'd called home with the man that promised to give her the world when all she wanted was his heart, she was regretful that she had ever agreed to meet him to sign the divorce papers. After fighting for so long and ignoring him they finally wanted the same thing; to end it all. She'd left in spring and now all the signs of autumn bloomed around the three bedroom ranch style home. Shutting off the engine she made no attempt to exit the vehicle. Their lives had changed drastically in the past few months and all of their family and friends were paying a price because of the whole sordid ordeal, but none more than little Joy.

Sitting on the bench on the porch was her soon to be ex-husband. Wearing a shirt that only added to his ripped biceps and six pack she knew he was still working out on a regular basis. Clearly neither of them knew what to do. It was their first time meeting face to face and alone in several weeks. After a few minutes he walked over to the car and opened his wife's car door.

"Hi Han."

"Hello Brice" was her monotone greeting.

Gravely he said, "Shall we go into the house?"

Without saying a word she took the lead when he motioned for her to walk ahead of him. He opened the door to what had been her home for the duration of their marriage. She'd picked out the furniture, the window treatments and the carpet. The new amenities in the kitchen were nothing short of the best. He promised to build her a home, but she chose to make the one they already had theirs, and so she had. Walking through the door an entire screen play was taking place in her head. The day she realized how much she loved him. Their marriage counseling that had taken place in that very living room. The first time she'd met his brothers. The first visit from Johanna. The day Miss. Ann showed up on their doorstep. The day Joy came come from the hospital. All destroyed in one afternoon.

"Look Brice, I have to be getting back so can we make this quick?"

"Whatever you say Hannah."

He was annoyed. Sitting on the couch he pulled the coffee table close enough for him to display the papers that his wife had given to him upon arrival.

"What is this Hannah? No child support and no visitation rights!! How could you and why? The only person you're hurting is our daughter. You can't make her stop loving me because you hate me. I'm not signing this!"

"Why Brice? What difference does it make? Why are you making this harder than it needs to be? All I want is out Brice, that's it. I don't want anything at all except my freedom. Anyway, these papers were drawn up a while ago. I won't keep her away from you anymore Brice. It does only hurt her and I don't want to hurt my baby. You're her daddy and you should be able to spend time with her. We just have to figure that out. I swear on my mother's grave you may be an active part of her life."

That statement almost floored him. She meant what she said he had no doubt. "Thank you Han, thank you so much. I really really miss her and," he choked up before he could finish. "Please, I want us. May we try again? I want our marriage."

"No, what you wanted was a woman in a polka dotted bra."

Grimacing at her remark he still came back with a quick, "Dumbest thing I have ever done. You were all I have ever wanted or needed. I wasn't thinking with the right head. I could keep apologizing from now until forever but somehow I don't think it will matter."

"No it wouldn't. Your words could never undo what has already been done."

Sighing he said, "I trust you to keep your word about visitations. You will receive child support and alimony and I will move out so my baby girl can move home to the only place she has ever lived. That is the only way I will agree to this."

"Your money doesn't mean anything to me Brice and I could never live in this house. Too many memories."

"This divorce is not what I want. I want my family back but I know I destroyed it with my own hand, my own actions. Maybe I have no right to still long for you and pray for my family, but I do more than anything in this world. I've gotten things right with God and with the other people that I disappointed. Now I just want things right with you Hannah Renee Corel-Waiters Chandler. Will you give me that chance?"

"If you wanted us so much why did you have the affair?"

"Stupid. I traded my wonderful reality for a fantasy. Han, I know I made a mistake. I remember every time I walk in this house and there is no one waiting for me. Each time I roll over at night and you aren't there I remember it. When I go into my daughter's room to check on her at night and she isn't there I realize what I have lost. When she doesn't jump in the bed with us on Saturday mornings, or run into my arms when I pick her up from daycare I know what I lost was my everything, my all and all." Moving closer to her he pushes the naturally curly hair away from her face. But she attempts to turn and walk away. Still, he reaches out to her by lovingly holding on to her hand.

"I didn't know what I had in you. I was so wrong to dishonor you and break our vows to one another."

"But you did and that can't be changed Brice."

"Can we start over Han? Please can we just start over?"

"It's not that simple Brice."

"I miss you so much. I miss our talks, your laugh, and just watching you sleep at night. I want us please Han."

"No Brice. If it didn't work the first time it won't work now. You know I'm not what you want. You should try and make it work with her."

"That was just an illusion and I was just plain dumb. I broke it off and transferred to a new office that same week."

He saw the pain reflecting in her eyes and frowned at what it looked like. His heart sank at the realization of just how much he had hurt her. She finally trusted someone, loved someone without reservation, and he was lucky enough to be that someone and he had thrown it all away.

"But it is all too real to me Brice."

"Forgive me. I know saying I'm sorry doesn't make it go away. But I really am sorry for all the pain I've caused you and our daughter."

He was a broken man and it was evident in his stance, his voice, and in his touch. She could feel him. For a moment the room was tranquil. He still held on to her hand. She was beautiful standing in the moonlight. She was more mature, a little thinner, and everything he could ever want, but he'd realized it too late. Neither of them knew why they stood in that moment of time. Nor did she understand why when he kissed her she didn't pull away, slap him, or anything besides kiss him back. She did not understand why she allowed him to undress her after carrying her to their bed. She didn't know why she believed him when he gruffly whispered in her ear repeatedly that he loved her. All she knew was that they wanted each other no matter how her mind told her to run, her heart continued in utter rebellion. He took his time going over every inch of her body interchanging with his hands and mouth. He wanted to please her, it was obvious and she did not want to fight him. When he took her hands and moved them to places he needed to be touched she was not shy about it. For the next hour they forget about the pending divorce, the betrayal, and the angry words that had been between them for so long. When they were both one in mind and body and pleasure was their only teacher they both screamed out in the moment, and that was when it all came rushing back.

Grabbing her clothes she took refuge in the restroom sobbing profusely. "How could you be so stupid?" She asked herself over and over as she hurriedly dressed. It took everything in her to ignore her husband's constant knocking and calling out to her on the other side of the door. Her mind continually tormented her with question after question. "Was it her or me he had just made love too?" "Why was it so good this time? Why did it have to feel so great? Why did it feel so good being in his arms again; touching him and him touching me?" She was scared, terrified and her heart hurt worse than it ever had. The tears fell to the restroom floor as she held on to the wall for support. She felt like someone was playing tug of war with her heart. Pulling it back and forth and with each move it was ripping causing excruciating pain to course through her body. "God what do I do she whispered to the walls. What do I do because I don't know? I feel his pain, but what about mine? How could I ever trust him again?

Why won't you help me stop loving him? How do I know he won't do it again? How do I move past his infidelity? Why do I love him so much? How could I still want my marriage? God please give me something so I will know what to do, please God, please."

When she finally opened the door he was sitting next to the restroom door on the floor in the hall. Slumped over like a rag doll ready to be dragged out with the trash. He looked up and as much as she told herself that she was going to exit quickly it just did not happen that way. Feeling like she was in a motion picture she slide down the wall beside him. Surprised, a tear trickled down his face. Still not knowing what her part was in the movie she put her head on his shoulder. They sat there in silence for a very long time until she spoke up.

"I told Connor about Joy." Silence filled the room. "Aren't you going to yell at me like everyone else did?"

"No. I know why you did it and I respect that. How did it go?"

"I really can't say. He was shocked, angry, and pretentiously hurt but how could I really know?"

"We will know in time."

"Could you live with him being a part of our lives?"

Looking at her with a glimmer of hope in his eyes he pulled her to him before answering. She had not realized it but she had referred to them as our, not mine or yours as she had so often in the previous six months. "We can handle it together. Summer Anna-Joy Chandler is my daughter and no one can take her away from me, from us."

"Brice."

"Yes Han."

"Just now, was it me you made love to or was it her? Do you still love her?"

"No Han. I don't love her. Truthfully I don't' know if I ever did. What I did is something I will always regret. Part of it was ego and the other lust. I've been finding out a lot about myself since beginning my counseling. I didn't know I had so many issues." He was looking directly into her face now. "May we try again? I need my wife and best friend; my family. I miss you so much Han. Just now it was only me and you, my wife, my lover, my friend."

"Brice I'm scared."

"So am I, but I'm scared of never being able to wake up with you lying next to me in the morning. Scared I won't get to put my daughter to bed after reading her a bed time story. Scared I will never get the opportunity to prove to you how sorry I am for what I did to us and show you how much I really love you. Give me that chance Han, please."

"Will you give me some time Brice?" She was shocked to hear the words come out of her mouth and even more dismayed when he said, "Yes." She knew all she really wanted was to come home so they could start all over again. She loved him in spite of his betrayal. She wanted them to be a family again maybe more than he did. She was learning through her study group that God was not only a Savior, but He was a Master at fixing things. She knew she should be headed back to her mother's home and to her baby but she remained seated next to her husband on the floor in the hall next to the restroom. He sensed something was up. He was becoming sensitive to her again.

"What do you need Han? Tell me what you need for me to do right now?"

Looking at him a bit thrown off by his sensitivity she still did not say anything. He did not push her. He'd known her long enough to be certain she would talk when ready. So they both waited. When she finally spoke several minutes later it was he who was surprised.

"Hold me tonight. Just me and you. No phones, no baby, no television, just us."

His heart leaped and he required no other motivation. Getting up from the floor he pulled her from the position they'd held for the past couple of hours. Slowly, methodically they walked down the hall to the bedroom. Sitting on the bed she sent her mother a text message about the baby and that was that. Brice walked into the bedroom and turned on the shower. When he reached for her moments later she took his hand and followed him. They did not speak. He put her hair back into a ponytail and began to massage her body with body wash ever so gently. Paying attention to every detail he spoke to her without opening his mouth. His hands spoke a language she understood, his eyes confirmed every word they said. When he'd dried her he put his bathrobe on her and they went to bed. She lay on his chest listening to his heartbeat and he held her tightly in his arms.

That was all she wanted. All she needed for the moment. It was the miracle he had asked God to give him.

At some time during the night her eyes pop open in horror. It was evident that she had suffered temporary insanity. Overcome with fear she made an attempt to maneuver out from under her husband's bear hold. Standing at the end of the bed wearing only the skin God had put her in she has begun to feel confused, embarrassed, stupid, and trounce with trepidation. Where were her clothes? What was she doing? Why would she give him permission to hurt her again? Nothing short of an emotional wreck she stood there until Brice suddenly realized she was no longer next to him and bolted from the bed.

"What's wrong honey? Talk to me."

By then she was shaking and tears that she had refused to cry for the past six months came pouring down.

"Are you cold?" No answer.

Brice doesn't know what to do. He knows what was taking place but was unprepared for the storm. Finding his bathrobe laying on the floor he put it on her and lead her back to the California king new England bed.

"Did I do something Brice? Just tell me if I did something to make you not want to be with me."

"Oh honey, please don't ever think that. I was just selfish. There is no other way to put it."

"Would you tell me if it happened again?"

"It's not going to happen again Han."

"But if it did, would you tell me?"

"Yes. I would tell you Han."

"Promise?"

"Promise." His attempts to kiss her tears away were futile. There were just too many. He knew he had caused them with his infidelity and inconsideration. She was more fragile now. More delicate than when she had first come running to him with her belly bump and confused heart. Instead of helping her by being the man he had made a covenant to be he became the person she had run from. The impact of just how much he'd damaged her was never clearer than that moment.

"Let's go back to bed honey."

All she said was "Okay" and followed his lead. It wasn't long before she drifted off to sleep again. Brice held her tight for the rest of the night while he prayed. He was going to be fine, but he knew it might be a long time before his wife would be alright again. God was the only one that could help her and he knew it. Just before dawn she spoke into the atmosphere. She knew he was awake by his heart rate and his breathing.

"I lost our baby Brice."

Confused he thinks she is talking about Joy so he says, "No she is fine. I checked on her before we went to bed and Johanna said she was in her bed with two of her dolls sleeping like a baby."

"No Brice I had a miscarriage. When I left I found out I was pregnant but I lost the baby. I wanted that baby so much. I needed something to hold on too, but it died anyway."

"When Han?"

"Three months ago. My body just couldn't carry him or her. I had a cyst and it cause complications with the pregnancy."

"Why didn't you tell me Han?"

"We weren't on speaking terms. I didn't think you cared."

"How could I not care about my child?"

"Not about the baby. About me, I didn't think it would have mattered once the baby was gone."

"God Han, I do care, I would have been there holding your hand."

"You can hold it now. I want my baby Brice."

"I'm so sorry I was out of place and you had to go through all that alone. How I wish everything would have worked out with the pregnancy."

"Do you think God was punishing me for keeping Joy away from you?"

"Not at all. God knows your heart Han and I just don't believe that is how He works."

"What are we going to do Brice?"

"Make it. We're going to make it one day at a time. If you are willing to give me another chance I know we can make it this time Han. Will you?"

She shook her head yes before going back to sleep. He was now wide awake and laden with sorrow for his wife and for the second child he would never have the opportunity to know, to father, or to love. Something inside him knew it was his fault. He caused the stress, the heartbreak, and pain that took their child. Over and over his heart screamed, "She just wasn't worth it."

Chapter 17

Hannah was now a stay at home wife and mother again. She followed her heart and went home to her husband and was eager to rebuild her family. She loved her husband and she wanted to believe that it was possible for him to fall in love with her again. Only it wasn't easy, some days she found it hard to even get out of bed. There were days she clung to Brice and others she hated the very sight of him. She had refused to go to counseling with him, but he continued. Some days she was just happy to be a family again, happy like in the beginning, and then there were the other days. The ones when she cried so much her eyes were puffy and swollen and her head hurt all day. The ones when she wasn't as patient with Joy and didn't answer the phone when the people that loved her called to check on her. When she did not want to comb her hair, brush her teeth, get dressed, eat and absolutely not go out anywhere, church included. Those days when she wanted to knock Brice over the head with the antique vase his mother had given them for their first Christmas as husband and wife. When she did not make dinner, would not say two words to her husband, and could not allow him to touch her. She hated those days.

Brice knew she was not herself and further blamed himself for her unhappiness. His work week was forty to sixty hours because of mandated overtime, but he still came home with a smile. He was happy because he had his wife again, despite her current state. His daughter that would usually greet him with hugs and kisses was happy to see him now because she was hungry or just wanted to go outside and play. He considered placing her in daycare but shuddered at what his wife may do if she wasn't at home. She had always been a remarkably strong person, but now her brokenness was evident. She cried a lot thinking he was unaware, but he knew. He knew her pain because he felt it. Her mother felt her pain, her brother felt her pain, and her best friends Jane and Michael; none knew how to help her. When Johanna tried to invite her to participate in things outside of the prison she had closed herself in to, she refused. When Jane tried to make her laugh she just fake smiled and thought of something to do. She rejected Michael's calls and always managed to miss her brother's. She took more sleeping pills than anyone was aware of and had a small bottle of alcohol hidden deep inside the closet that she frequented more and more. Hannah Renee Corel-Waiters Chandler had fallen apart.

Young Hannah had resurfaced again and she was wreaking havoc in her life. She was liable to show up anywhere, at any time without notice or invitation. During her adolescent, tween and teenage years she had been able to contain or at least redirect her anger but she no longer had control of the little girl that should have died when she started her new life with Brice and with God. Young, bitter, weary and worn Hannah said do unto others as they have done to you. Yes, it was wrong, but it felt good, for a little while anyway. Then she thought about how far she had come and how that behavior hurt the people that did care for her and the guilt she carried made her even angrier. As soon as she made up her mind that she was going to change and let her past go something else happened and she exploded again. Her mother would say something and she would not speak to her for a few days. How was she supposed to have the answers to life? Johanna may have had a direct line to God but she did not. Then Jane was constantly trying to get her out somewhere to do something and she would have to set her straight. Michael was good to her, no doubt about it, but he just did not understand so she'd had to swear off certain conversations, especially about the men in her life. What else was there to converse about? For some reason he didn't like any of the men in her life. Bob she tolerated, he was a gentle, kind man and the only thing that helped her day was receiving his encouraging text messages. Maybe because he wasn't trying to tell her what to do or control her life, he just gave the best part of him and never asked for anything in return. He was the only exception. The neighbors got on her nerves, the mailman, the people at the super market, and even the weather.

It wasn't rocket science; something was eating at her because she was the only common denominator. There was a possibility it was the husband she loved and hated. The fact that Connor had not cared that he was a father, just like her father hadn't. There was the unemployment thing she had going on, not liking the church she was a member of, it had been her mother's choice and she had been out numbered when Brice agreed with her. She needed a place that taught a little slower so she could grasp what she was supposed to do and with a lot less noise. At least while the speaker was orating. There was that mother thing. The one that had given up her life in Washington, retired from her job, and loved her unconditionally, but she was sure she was an awful daughter in return. What if she grew to resent her? Or if she decided she wasn't worth sticking around for and left? She still longed for the child that she was never going to see or hold. Then there was the thing she had not been able to share with anyone at all; not even God. It hurt too much and it could destroy her and the marriage she was making too less of an attempt to save. That was a day in the life of Hannah and she was tired of her own story. On the rare occasion she had a good day, it wasn't lasting.

It was Monday morning again. She hated Mondays. Brice went to work for another long week and she was left with the mean bitter person living inside her. Already she and Joy had battled about the breakfast she didn't want to eat and why her daddy left her again. When her brother phones just after nine she doesn't make an attempt to answer the phone. When Joy brings her the phone she decided to listen to his message.

"Hi Hannah Banana This is your big brother calling. We should talk, soon. Call me, Tobias." Decoding a message from her brother wasn't hard. He talked when he had something on his mind. Something was up. Having no strength to handle one more thing she ignored his wish for a return call.

Just after lunch there was a fierce knock on the door that both puzzled and annoyed the depressed wife and mother. All attempts to ignore the constant knocking and ringing of the doorbell were futile. With attitude she finally flung open the door and doesn't get a chance to say a word before Jane waltzed in and announced, "Because you are my friend and I know and you know, Chile you have some issues and I do not want to have to put a good old fashion Cajun beating on you I have signed both of us up for kick boxing classes. Call it intervention between the obvious two people you have become, Mrs. Mad as hades and Sister mean and hateful. Call it prevention so that you don't end up doing time because you beat up the bagger at the grocery store, the usher at the church, Brice…; either way, you are going."

"Must you be so asinine on a Monday?"

"So now you are cussing me, huh?"

"Hardly, but you are insulting me, JEN NI FER, so why don't you do me a favor and find someone who needs your assistance, because I am just fine." With that she goes to the couch and sits on it displaying her annoyance.

"Say what you will but you need help and like it or not you are going to get it. I know you, and you are on the edge and I refuse to sit around until you fall off and break your stubborn neck HANNAH!"

"I don't know what you are talking about. My life is great. What could I have to be upset about Jane, tell me, what?"

"First off, you need to check that tone with me because I could have just slipped you some of those pills that make you happy from those commercials. Never mind if you grew hair on your chest afterwards or thought you could fly, I would still love you. Even when you act like you need an exorcism performed, I still love you. You are my sister and I have made a solemn promise to God that I would not shoot relatives, unless it's Junior or Cret and then it would only be in the foot so it would slow them down when they are running off into the woods with people's stuff. The way I figure it this is the best way."

Hannah screamed in exasperation and then picked up a pillow from the sofa and tossed it at her best friend. "Cret and Junior Jane, really, do you get your relatives through mail order?" Jane catches the pillow and says, "You throw like a girl. One more reason you need this kick boxing class."

"Alright already! I will go if you just shut up about it."

"Great, be ready at four. Your mother has agreed to watch the baby, and I know Brice is working overtime tonight so no excuses."

"My my aren't you just the efficient one? You just forgot I need ample time to prepare dinner for my family."

"Right…like that is something you would actually do these days. I will be back at 3:30 this afternoon and you had better be ready."

"Ha! You are not the boss of me." Smirking she waved to her friend as she watched her back out of her drive way.

By the time Jane made her second appearance of the day Joy had eaten snack and was happily drawing at the kitchen table while her grandmother prepared the dinner she insisted on making for her family. Hannah was actually looking forward to the kick boxing class. During her entire stay in Washington she'd always had gym partners. Odd she never thought of it being a subconscious therapy or stress reducer. Since getting married she had only walked when her schedule or weather permitted. When she left Brice she gave up on any kind of work out regiment. The constant warring in her heart were all she could handle. Needless to say she was looking forward to getting physical.

Jane was all smiles once she saw the instructor for the class. The would be half Italian, half god looked like someone had just sculptured him that very morning. His perfectly bronze 6' something body was flawless in every way. There was no amazement that the class was ninety-nine percent female. Purring like a cat Jane says, "Be still my heart, he is totally gorgeous."

As dry as it could have been said Hannah replies, "Totally." The next hour quickly went from being comical to hilarious, to downright shameful as her sister friend flaunts, flirts, and feels up the instructor. When that doesn't work she becomes helpless and needs extra assistance for every move. "Hannah whispers to her, "Wonder what your church boy would think of you now?"

"He is engaged to the pastor's daughter my dear."

Now that was a bomb shell to Hannah and she knew it had been for Jane who was attempting to play it down. "Apparently we both need this class my sister."

"Clearly" was all she said but they both understood it wasn't the time or the place. Hannah had a mirror image of her selflessness. Jane was in her own crisis and she had been none the wiser. On the drive home Hannah revisits the subject. "What happened Jane?"

"Don't really know, but either way it started wrong so I knew it would end wrong."

"Do you love him?"

"Doesn't matter, he's not mine to love anymore. I guess he never really was to begin with." Her matter of fact tone concerned Hannah but she had enough trouble of her own to dare think she was capable of helping someone else through theirs. The two ride in silence the remainder of the trip back to Hannah's home.

"Mommy!" Joy was to her feet the instant the door opened. She loved her Mommy and that was one of the greatest miracles and mysteries in the world to Hannah. Picking her up she swings her around and around kissing her over and over again to Joy's delight. Then it was Aunt Jane's turn to give her butterfly kisses and be the tickle monster. Johanna watched from a distance. She hoped all the noise was a sign that her daughter was in a better mood.

"Hi Mommy, dinner smells delicious. Thanks for preparing it." Hannah doesn't make eye contact with her mother. She felt like she was constantly being scrutinized and how could she compete with God. He was always showing her mother something, but the truth was, she did not always want to hear about it.

"Anytime" was her only comment and she continued to set the table. Hannah not wanting to be alone with her has a moment of genius. "Jane you should stay for dinner."

Jane who was on to her little game gives her the "I will get you for this later" look and graciously accepts. When Johanna asks, "Will Brice be working overtime tonight Baby Girl?" Hannah wanted to say mind your business Mom, but smiled and said, "I believe so Mother." Her tone and the fact that she referred to her as Mother was like telling Johanna to back off and mind your own business in a nice but naughty way. The truth that her mother was incorrigible did not help matters. She meant well but at times it was exhausting. Brice was the last thing on her mind. He would find his way home eventually, plus he was an educated adult male and could fend for himself.

"Well I will just place dinner in the microwave for him then."

"That's great, thank you so much." Hannah deceived no one with her perfect answers. Jane texts her a little note saying, "You would never win any award with that horrid acting." Hannah just ignored her and prepared Joy for dinner.

Baked Ziti was a household favorite and it was one of the rare days Hannah actually had an appetite. The three made small talk about nothing in general. Joy was the center of attention as usual and that lightened the atmosphere. It wasn't until they were doing cleanup that the Mr. made his appearance. Hannah pretended to be engrossed with loading the dishwasher. When her husband gave a general greeting, picked up his daughter, then made his way over to give her a hello kiss she avoids him by putting the dinner from the microwave between them. "You must be hungry. Have a seat and I'll get you something to drink." Jane and Johanna both observed the cold shoulder she gave him. Both see it as a perfect time to make their exit. After they left there was little or no communication between them. He spent time with his daughter and she took refuge in a book. He wanted to talk, she did not. He needed to touch her, she thought he was repulsive. The next few days passed much the same way, minus the dinner being prepared for him.

Chapter 18

The holidays were fast approaching and Hannah grew gloomier by the day. She had started to believe there was some validity to the seasonal depression she always heard about during the holidays. Apparently her own sadness had met with the holiday blues and had a baby and she was catching it trying to keep it quiet. Not knowing what to do most days she did nothing. What she wanted in life vacillated from day to day. She did know she did not want to see anyone with the last name Chandler; Joy being the only exception, during Thanksgiving. Brice was included in that number on a bad day. Sometimes she was just hopeless. She believed she had fought all of her life for the dream of a good life, but now she knew that was mere fantasy. When you do what's right things don't always get better or turn out well. Her dead mother was a perfect example. You can give your all and end up with nothing at all. She didn't like those kinds of equations and being as analytical as she was it messed with her mind; a lot too much.

When her husband informs her that they were to spend Thanksgiving Day with his parents she looked at him with such an evil that he cringed. "You, Brice Anthony Chandler may have dinner anywhere you wish to have it Thanksgiving or any other day, but I will not be in attendance."

"Why would you say such a thing Han?"

"Do you really need to ask? Everyone and I do mean everyone knows your mother does not like me, Jesus included. She was happy when we split and further more let people far and near know that it was entirely my fault. Knowing that it was her precious son that brought someone else into our marriage she still said, and I quote, "If I had been taking care of home you wouldn't have had to go outside of the home." She said that I was just reaping what I sowed when I killed her grandbaby, something only you could have told her about. Now not only am I a whore, but word on the street is baby killer has been added to my rap sheet. Not to mention her soon to be ex-daughter in law so you can find the wife God intended her Toni bear to have!"

"No I did not tell her any such thing." The vein in his neck was protruding and his jaw clenched; a clear sign that he was angry.

"You are such a compulsive liar Brice. How else could she know? I certainly did not tell her. Your mother would be the last person on earth that I would ever tell anything with her judgmental, nose in the air, I'm better than all of you, self!"

"God you are so mean Hannah! Why are you so spiteful?"

"You made me this way" she says storming from the bedroom slamming the door behind her. The noise rattled Joy and Brice's soul, but she didn't care. Entering the room that used to be a computer slash office, the room where she found him on video call with his mistress, she slammed that door too and then locked it. He knows she will probably spend the night there. Gathering up his little girl he consoled her by singing her favorite song and she goes back to sleep. He finds a room of his own to be alone. There he cried like he was told by his mother and his father that no man should ever do. He was at a lost for what else to do. Up until the last hour of his life he always felt he could confide in his father. He knew exactly how his mother got the information about the abortion, his dad. That was the only person he had ever uttered a word to; that trust was now broken along with his marriage and he was giving up hope of it ever being repaired.

While Hannah sat on the floor sipping her wine in the room of lust as she had so named it, she regretted ever returning to San Antonio. She regretted marrying Brice Chandler, and most of all she regretted what she had become. It was in that half sober, half alive, half insane moment that once again she heard the voice. "You will find forgiveness when you learn how to forgive. Go to your mother, she needs you. There you will receive your healing as you go and as you obey. Healing for your marriage and your family. You won't go alone because I will be with you."

Tiredly she spoke into the air, "But why, why do I have to be the one. Why is it that you require so much of me yet you let these people treat me any kind of way and get away with it. Why am I everyone's punching bag? Can't I fight back? Why can't I hurt them just like they hurt me? She doesn't deserve forgiveness and neither does Brice. They were adults and they knew what they were doing so let them suffer just like I have had to at their hands."

"This is about you Hannah. If you allow me to I will heal you and all those around you."

Still unconvinced she argues, "How do I know this is even real and not some reaction to this alcohol? Even in the hospital how can I be sure that it wasn't the medication and the grief making me hear and see things? I used to know when I was hearing from you. I used to know things before they happen but not anymore. Disappointment is all I know now. I hate life most days because I feel like I am sitting on the sidelines watching people live but I just don't know how to anymore. Why didn't I know what Brice was doing? How is it that I was so blind?"

"You must trust me and you will learn to trust your husband again."

"Is that it? You have to give me something, please I need something."

"Go to your husband Hannah. When you lay with him he will put his arms around you and this is what he will say to you…'I love you Han. Please forgive me for betraying your trust in me about our marriage and about the abortion. It will never happen again, I swear on my life.' This is how you will know. Then he will kiss you. Not on the mouth or forehead as you are accustomed, but on your hands as he recites your wedding vows in a renewal to you and your marriage. Go to him."

She gets up and takes the wine to the kitchen sink and pours it down the drain and disposes the empty bottle. Next she brushed her teeth and pulled her hair into a ponytail before showering. She then checked on her little girl who was sucking on her thumb, something she only did when she was afraid. She resisted the urge to take her from her bed and just hold her but thought it better that she get a good night's sleep. Petrified and still hurting she finally made her way to the bedroom where her husband was straddled across their bed on his back staring up at the ceiling.

When she enters the room he doesn't move. He doesn't know what to expect. So he braced himself for the fight that was never ending and became bitter and bitter with each round it went. He just wanted peace, a little love, and one day her forgiveness. Maybe that wasn't going to be possible for them. The reality felt like a dagger to his heart. He was cognizant firsthand what resentment looked like and he saw it each day in his wife. He felt it when he tried to touch her on any level and for him it had become harder and harder to face. Watching her he wondered what she was about to say to him, do to him, or throw at him. She hesitated and looked a little embarrassed, even a little frightened like she was trying to convince herself of something.

To him she was beautiful, even on her worse day she was gorgeous. It didn't matter how she wore her hair, it didn't matter what she wore, it didn't matter if she smiled or frowned, Hannah Renee was stunning to him. He loved his wife more now than before. He missed the witty, thoughtful, playful, genius of a wife he said I do to. The one that had the strength and will power that surpassed that of ordinary people. The fighter, go getter, make a masterpiece out of a mess, I don't need much, just your love. The same love that he knew he'd violated and compromised. He needed her so badly it made him sick. He longed for the days of stolen kisses and long nights of love making. When she pretended to be the maid, the stripper and even the naughty nun. The times she stepped off the elevator on his job, picnic basket in hand looking like she was out of a magazine. The times she planned family time for the three of them. Friday night games of strip poker. Saturday morning stolen kisses and serving him breakfast in her bikini. He missed the talks about their future and the children they would add to their family. He craved the days when work was gruesome and all he had to do was call and hear the sound of her voice and everything was better. Looking across a room and watching her when she wasn't looking and thinking he was the luckiest man in the world. Feeling when she stepped into the room because the atmosphere changed when she entered was a dream come true.

Lost somewhere in thought or fantasy the movement on the bed made him snap back to reality. His wife was there beside him. Careful to leave no space between them she'd eased as close to him as she could position herself on her back next to him. Neither of them spoke. He didn't know what made her come; he wasn't overly concern about it, he was just happy to hold her again. That she allowed him to touch her again. It was an answer to his prayers. The sign he'd prayed for and the little bit of hope he needed to give him strength to hold on and continue to fight for his family. Rolling onto his side he looked in her eyes. She stared up at him but still did not speak. Leaning on his elbow He touched her hair. He had always been a hair man. Stroking her wet curls he hoped he was not dreaming. Since that day she'd come to have him sign the divorce papers they had not been intimate. He longed for the right words to tell her, to help her heal so they could start over. He wanted to see the look she used to get when he came home from work or across a crowded room. He had once been her world, he captured her heart once and he prayed for a chance to have it again.

She stared at him but still would not speak. Torn between the anger and her unforgiving heart she searched his face for anything that would tell her it was safe to trust him again. Just when doubt was about to set in about the message she was certain came from God, her husband touched her. His hand caressed her arm at first and then continued down to her hand. He kissed each one, slowly, purposefully and gently; first the right then the left. Her heartbeat instantly became rapid.

"I love you Han. Please forgive me for betraying your trust in me about our marriage and about the abortion. It will never happen again, I swear on my life. I need you and I want us. Today, right now I make a new commitment to our marriage that only death will stop me from keeping."

Getting in a kneeling position on their bed he drew her up towards him and said, "I, Brice Anthony Chandler, take you, Hannah Renee Corel-Waiters Chandler to be my wife, to have and to hold from this day forward, for better or for worse, for richer, for poorer, in sickness and in health, to love and to cherish; from this day forward until death do us part."

Each word was like medicine to her heart because she knew God backed them. Now she knew it had been God that spoke to her while in the hospital and in that room. Relieved, excited and ready to be Mrs. Brice Chandler again she pounced on him. He wasn't prepared, boy was he not prepared. The sudden surprise attack threw him off balance and they both fell off the bed. He didn't know what was going on and lay stunned until she kissed him long and hard. When he took his hand and pushed her away Hannah was immediately offended. He needed to see her eyes because they had always told her story. He lifted her head which was down in disappointment but she pulled away and tried to get up and leave the room. "No baby, no, please don't leave, I just want to look at you."

His voice was different and she wondered why. Her curiosity was enough for him to look into her eyes long enough to realize that she wanted him, them. This time it was he who kissed her. Not knowing what was going on, a confused Hannah was not so willing until her husband flipped her over onto the carpeted bedroom floor and once again consummated their vows. It was a long time before either of their breathing regulated. He held his wife close and she accepted all the love he was willing to give her. When he picked her up and placed her under the duvet she still had not spoken. All she wanted was to enjoy those moments. It had been so long since they had truly been together. She knew first hand you could have sex and love had nothing to do with it, and then she was well aware that you could be taken to a place in love making that only heaven could define. That night was one of those times and she wanted to relish every moment. Not wanting to say the wrong thing she said nothing. Not wanting to misinterpret incorrectly what he said when he attempted to speak she put her finger over his mouth and silenced him. When she put her head on his chest he was satisfied to just hold her and that was how they fell asleep.

Chapter 19

The kitchen was where Brice Chandler found his wife the following morning. Sure he had overslept it surprised him to see the clock on the microwave say six in the morning. He had slept restlessly for almost eight months, but that morning he was not carrying the burdens that plagued him for so long. Breakfast was made and she had ironed his clothing for the next couple of days of the work week and the following week. She didn't see him standing in the door watching her. She wore a red pair of boy shorts and a matching lace camisole. Her hair was brushed into a ponytail and her feet graced in white designer slippers. Wearing no make-up or jewelry she looked more like a teenager than the twenty-four year old woman she was. Her caramel skin was flawless and although smaller than usual her size six frame was still perfect for him. His heart saddened just briefly as he questioned his own infidelity. How could he have hurt her so, them so? She deserved better. Turning she sees him in the doorway and smiled. He knew she was her old self again. Only she would be happy at that hour in the morning.

"Morning" he says walking over to her and putting his arms around her.

"Good morning Mr. Chandler. How does bacon, eggs, and toast sound?"

"Wonderful Mrs. Chandler, just wonderful." Kissing her on the mouth he doesn't want to let her go. She whispers in his ear, "You have to loosen your hold so I may serve you silly." Still he holds her to the point that she readjusts herself to get a better look at him. That was when she discovered that he had awakened with a hearty appetite and she was ready to give him what he wanted. Nibbling on his ear she tells him that she wants precisely what he wants. He in turn removes the tie from her hair and it falls around her shoulders. He kisses her on the neck, then a little lower and a little lower. By then she has opened his bathrobe and was exploring the body she loved so much. He tells her over and over again he loves her and how much he needs her. The more he says it the more aroused she becomes and began to lead him into places she knew he loved to rediscover. Just when she thought she was in charge he picks her up and puts her on the kitchen counter and had it not been for the passionate kissing she was sure her display of pleasure could have been heard by the neighbors. "Oh Brice I missed you so much." He hoped that she would have said she loved him, but that would come in time as she learned to trust him again. Her slippers were somewhere in the room and so was his bathrobe. Again she broke the silence, "Brice can we go away for a few days? Just us; me, you and Joy?"

"I would like that very much Han." That made her happy. She wanted to talk to him about the things that took place when they were apart. She wanted to hear about the counseling he was attending faithfully, and she needed to do some confessing of her own. Still standing in the kitchen holding tightly to one another, his face on her chest and her head resting on his head they resent the clock on the wall that dictated that they must be separated soon so he could get to work on time. It was Thursday and that meant he would be working late. Fridays had been a half work day for him but the holidays always demanded ten to twelve hour days five times a week.

"What about this weekend?" When he said it she couldn't believe her ears. She'd figured their trip would have to be some time after the New Year with his taxing schedule and Thanksgiving being only two weeks away.

"Really!" her voice could not conceal her excitement.

"You plan the trip and I will make sure everything else is taken care of and when I get off work on Friday afternoon it's a family road trip."

Squealing she hugs and kisses him. She was smiling so hard her eyes twinkled. He loved to see them that way and he loved knowing that he was the reason for it.

By the time the Chandler family hit the interstate on Friday evening headed to a hideaway in Austin neither of them could wait to shut out the world if only for a couple of days. Her mother hopelessly tried to convince her to leave Joy with her so they could spend some time as a couple but it was not what either of them wanted. They were a family that still needed much healing and Joy was a part of that healing.

The commute was relatively quiet. Each family member engrossed in their own world. Brice gave careful attention to the highway due to dense fog. Hannah text back and forth between Jane and Michael; and Joy found her own amusement. She loved tall buildings and city lights and was content to observe the passing buildings give way to the dark starlit cascade above them and a never-ending highway ahead.

Hannah, now done with her phone, mutters over how she was going to begin her confessions to her husband. Her news would be the true test of whether their marriage would be able to be reconciled. All she wanted was rest and was ready to call a cease fire from the previous months of intense battle. It was arduous work making a cheating husband make restitution for his betrayal; more than she had the strength or the hatred to continue to carry out.

During the one hour and fifteen minute drive each chance her husband got to touch her hand, her thigh or her hair he took. Not wanting to be a limp noodle she reassured him by giving him a love squeeze periodically, but she really just longed to nap during the remainder of the trip. Joy had been up several times during the previous night; having fallen prey to the San Antonio weather. The tug of war between hot and cold had tossed her little immune system into utter confusion. The allergies ignited the asthma and thus the breathing treatments were again her best friend. That is besides her dolls, Ms. Daisy, Ms. Bella, and of course Jimmy who were all securely strapped in their seatbelts in the back seat. She considered rescheduling the trip but tossed the idea when she thought of how much they all needed to get away.

When the words, "I love you" drift into the stagnant atmosphere they were almost intrusive. It seemed harsh not to answer them, but she doesn't. He turns and amid the darkness is relieved to see the soft smile on her face and was content once more. "You okay Han?" Wanting nothing more than serenity she answers because she knows he is searching. "Just tired" was her only reply. God and she knew it was the gospel truth, she hoped he did too.

"Well maybe you can get some much needed rest this weekend. By the way, I made an appointment for you to have a one hour massage in the morning. That includes a facial, manicure and a pedicure. My queen needs to be pampered."

"Oh Brice how sweet." She hoped he bought into her deception. All she really wanted was for the three of them to do nothing together. When he gives his, I impressed you smile, she knew she had weaved her little web. When she was certain Joy was asleep in the back seat she just has to get one of her secrets off her chest. "Brice." He knew by the way she said his name he wasn't going to like what was coming next.

"Yes Love."

"I need to tell you something." She was a bit nervous and couldn't understand why but it was evident in her voice.

"Why don't we talk about it later?"

She was aware of what he was trying to do but ignored him. "Now is a good time I think."

"Alright then, let's talk."

Turning to look at him she takes a breath and begins. "When we were separated, when I visited my brother, I did something of which I am not proud."

Fist clenched on the steering wheel, keeping his eyes on the road, through tight lips he says, "Explain."

"Well…, I kissed another man. He touched me, we kissed, and…"

He interrupts with a stern, "Who."

"Does it matter Brice? I mean really, I just wanted you to know that it happened."

"Yes it matters. Where did he touch you? Did you sleep with him?"

"Dr. Emmanuel Brice and no I did not sleep with him. Again, we were separated and it was only a kiss."

"No it wasn't only a kiss. If it had been you wouldn't feel the need to tell me about it. I know you Han. Did you want to sleep with him?"

"Brice please, stop. What I wanted was you, my husband, my friend, the father of my children, but you know that story better than I do."

"Did you want him Han? Please tell me the truth."

"If you're asking if I wanted to be made love to then the answer is yes. Yes I wanted to be touched, to be told I was beautiful, to believe that someone could desire me, but he wasn't the one that I needed to do those things. Can you understand that Brice? I felt so ugly, so worthless and unloved." For a while they ride in silence. Then he reaches out and grabs her hand and holds it for the last few miles of the trip.

By the time they are checked into The Chalet, grab a bite to eat and administer Joy her medications it is already after eight, which felt more like midnight to Hannah. The plans she had for debuting her little waitress outfit with the peek-a-boo top that left little to the imagination while wearing her stiletto heels were abandoned. Holding her sleeping daughter she doses on the couch while her husband looks on from the chair. She sees the disappointment in his demeanor and it is solidified in his actions when he announces he was going to take a shower. She knows she is sending mixed signals to him. She was the one that asked for the trip and made the plans.

Putting Joy in the bed across from theirs she decides to put her feelings aside and be a wife to her ailing husband. Standing in the bathroom mirror she strips down to the way he liked her best, to include removing the hair clips that held her hair style neatly in place. Brice was a hair man and would prefer her hair to fall freely down her back and this trip was about giving him what he wanted. Adding the red lip gloss from her pants pocket that now lay in the floor she shakes off the feelings of exhaustion. When she slips through the door of the shower her husband is clearly surprised but says not a word and neither does she.

Taking the cloth from him and putting it aside she pours body wash in her hands and begin to massage it first onto his chest and then downward. His eyes never leave hers. Still there are no words spoken but the conversation is intense. She moves her hands across his body to places that make him want to scream out. His hands are running through her wet curls and by now he has to be a participant. Kissing her on the neck he whispers in her ear how much he loves her, how much he needs her, and how beautiful she is. Now she is aroused. Pushing him down she forces him to sit on the little shower bench so she can straddle him but he can't stay there. He needs to be in control and when he was her heart skipped a beat because she was never disappointed. Picking her up he uses the shower wall to give him leverage and takes command. Now she moans and groans while calling out his name. That was what he wanted.

"You are my wife Hannah, my wife. No one else gets to touch you, no one. He is a little rough and his body tense as he kisses her. Their tongues tangle and their bodies create a riot in the water. "Say it Han" he demands, "I need to hear you say it."

"I love you Brice, God I love you so much it hurts", she manages to get out before he takes her to a new place in love making and she collapses in his arms.

Turning off the water he wraps her in a towel, puts on a bathrobe and carries her to their bed. Pulling back the covers he places her in the middle of the queen sized bed and then joins her. He wants to hold her. He needs to hold her and she doesn't object. Lying on his chest listening to the sound of his heart she reaches out and takes his right hand in her left hand and they lay listening to the sounds of the quiet country hideaway. Sometime later he asks, "Did I hurt you? I didn't mean to if I did." She doesn't want to talk but knows he needs an answer so she shakes her head, "No" so they can go back to the new peace she was beginning to embrace. Truth was she liked the new Brice. The take charge, rough around the edges man he was becoming. It was a turn on to her and even though she would never say it out loud she needed a bad boy in her bed if no other place.

Later, just to see if he would play into her hands she blows into his ear and says, "I love you Mr. Chandler and no one can make me hot and bothered the way you do." She feels him immediately rise to the occasion. Flipping her over in the bed he makes her remember just how much she wanted their marriage to have a new beginning.

Chapter 20

Bright and early the next morning Joy, who was now well rested, wakes her parents by jumping up and down and singing very loudly. "Wake up, wake up, it's time to wake! Get out of bed and enjoy this day, learn new things, laugh and play, it's time to wake up!"

Turning over to face her husband Hannah says, "That is your child" and the proud father replies, "You're darn skippy she's all mine" and starts a game of tickle monster with his daughter. Joy laughs until she has a bout of coughing and then her daddy scoops her up and gives her a breathing treatment. During the treatment he makes up a story about a little princess named Summer. Joy fills in the details of the story each time he pauses. Of course this little princess was the smartest in the land, the prettiest of all, and she has magical powers that turn all sad faces into happy ones just by walking into a room.

Hannah looks on. The relationship between the two is all she could have ever wished for her daughter. She saddens momentarily when she thinks of all the sorrow inflicted on her Joy by keeping the two apart. She knew the residue of that heartache was still very much a part of their lives each time Brice left the house for any reason and she cried fearing he wouldn't return. When she had to hold his hand just to fall asleep at night because she thought that would make him still be there the next morning. They both loved him; she only wished he understood just how much.

After watching public television with their daughter, playing a game of tag with her, and feasting on fresh fruit and cereal bars, the family ventures to the great outdoors. According to the clerk at The Chalet, there was a kiddie carnival downtown. It was the perfect thing to do while Mrs. Chandler went to the spa.

Once the pedicure and manicure were completed Hannah finds herself on the table, naked with the exception of a towel, ready for her massage. She was happy that her husband had given her such a gift. Not knowing just how fatigued she was, she drifted off to sleep almost immediately; thus the dream.

Languished she saw Miss. Ann laying on a gurney of some sort. In the dark windowless room there stood only a bed, one nightstand, and four bare white padded walls. The stint of the room was almost unbearable; fusty and rigor mortis dance on the wall she lay staring onto. IV poles line the entire right side of the bed. She was a shell; her bones quite visible. Her face sunken with no flesh to hold it together she resembled the Halloween masks Hannah hated to see on the shelves.

Suddenly from beneath the white sheet a hand evolves slowly reaching in Hannah's direction. Stoic she looks on. She knows that Miss. Ann is bidding her to come but she is frozen. In agreement with the hand her eyes entreat Hannah but she can't, or won't. After doing this numerous times with the same response, the hand finally collapses lifeless hitting the metal bar on the bed shattering the gold watch that was on its wrist. The room suddenly fills with people who immediately begin to unhook the machines. After tagging her toe her face is covered with a white sheet. Men appear to roll her away, but just before the last part of the bed is out of the door the part of the sheet that is covering her foot falls away and the letters on the tag identifying her are visible. Instead of her name, it read, guilt.

She begins to scream, "Mom! Mom! Mom!" but Miss. Ann does not respond. Pushing the attendees out of her way she pulls back the cover and get as close to her face as possible still screaming, "Mom! Mom! I forgive you Mom! Mom!" Nothing. Someone takes her hand, she doesn't know who, and pulls her aside so the bed can roll away. When the doors swing closed behind the bed there Hannah stands with a heart that feels like it had exploded within her chest. Pain seizes her head and heart and she lets out a shrill.

That's what woke her and frightened the masseuse half to death. The poor girl did not know what to make of the situation. Her green eyes looked troubled and Hannah could tell she was trying to find something to do to make the situation better. After the scream, followed by the intimate time with the waste basket, the young woman offered her water in a crystal wine glass. Taking small sips sitting on the side of the table the young girl stays at her side.

"Mrs. Chandler, may I call someone" she asks with a heavy Texan accent.

"No, I'll be fine. Thank you. Probably something I ate. I think I'll just get dressed and wait for my husband in the lounge." In Hannah's heart she knew she was as troubled as a mobile home during a tornado, but how could voicing her fears help anything?

The girl, still red as a beet, says, "Sometimes the toxins can cause different reactions to your body."

"No, Misty, you were awesome. The next time I am in town I will look you up."

That brought a smile to her face. "Well I will be just out front if you need me Mrs. Chandler" and with that she was gone.

Hannah pretended not to see Misty peering in the room often to check on her client. She just wanted to get out of there and leave the whole ordeal behind her. That was a fantasy of course because trouble was packed and ready to move whenever she moved, getaway or not. By the time Brice and Joy arrived she felt worse and she could not conceal it.

Brice took one look at her and knew something was wrong. "What's wrong?" He was speaking while walking to the desk to get whatever took place rectified. Taking his hand, Hannah leads him away whispering, "No please Brice, don't. That's not it."

"You better tell me something because I am certain you are not just fine and I want to know who is responsible so I can check them." His display of anger was not becoming.

"Later baby, I will tell you when you and I can talk privately." Kissing him on the lips she smiled and continued, "Thank you for the pampering, it was delightful, just splendid.

"Then what was the look I saw? Don't say it wasn't anything because I know it was a big something Han, I know."

The new husband since the reconciliation would not permit her to leave him to guess, so she told him, "I had a dream Brice. I really want to tell you about it when we have no distractions, let alone an audience. Can you give me this one, please?"

Her heart was heavy as demonstrated in her countenance and she knew it. Warring with so many emotions, so much pain, and too few answers was sucking the life from her. Her mother always told her as a little girl that a hard head would make a soft behind and at the moment her buttocks felt raw. Disobedience was the only reason for it and she knew it. In the dream she'd called Miss. Ann Mom and had felt raw emotion when she realized it was too late to ever truly tell her she was forgiven. Never had she ever considered Miss. Ann as a person at any point during her life. To Hannah, Antoinette Rachel Hardy was a monster; inhuman and deserving of the hell fire so many preachers on television often spoke about. Some called her Ann, others Angela, her mother had called her Ella, but she personally called her Satan. Since she had come from her womb what that made her was another underlining issue?

Her mind flooded with all those times she just wanted a life of her own. She longed for the people to pay for the things that had been so willingly done to her. She'd always dismissed the possibilities of those people being victims somehow themselves. The Miss Ann lying on that bed was not the one that had been given custody of her when her mother died. She looked the same, but in her heart Hannah knew she was not that person. It reflected in the eyes that begged her to take her hand, she was sure something had changed. That was why the dream had been so devastating. Something in her wanted to know, desperately needed to know that person, if only to forgive her and allow her to forgive herself. Guilt was a flesh eating disease that the only cure was forgiveness. She knew that now. She finally understood what God had been trying to tell her for so long.

Again, she asked the husband she loved so much, delicately brushing her hand over his shoulder, "Will you Brice? I do want to tell you everything." He did not answer right away. They walked to the car, secured their daughter in her car seat and had driven a few blocks before he said, "I want to know everything before we get back to San Antonio. No more secrets Han."

Nodding her head she agreed to his terms. She was unsure how her emotions should be at that point about his take charge attitude. What on earth was he being told in his counseling sessions? The mean girl in her wanted to tell him some things she hoped Jesus would cover His ears so she

126

could say them. Really, no more secrets you….she reels her mind in. It was only for a few seconds then it was running away again thinking how dare he tell me such foolishness after all he…she was in a full blown argument with him in her head before she realized they were back at their room.

"Mommy, pick me up Mommy" little Joy said repeatedly. She turned around and her daughter and her husband were staring at her. Cursing in her mind she was most assured that incident would be yet another conversation later. When she opened the door to their room there was a boutique of flowers sitting on the little table along with a picnic basket. Surprised, she turned to ask her husband about it, but he had disappeared.

Joy was filled to capacity with carnival food, not a good thing, and was ready for her afternoon nap. It was perfect timing for them. After putting their daughter down for her nap she goes in search of her husband. She finds him sitting on the veranda. He does not look up when she steps outside. All she wanted was peace, a little love, and as normal a life as possible; she needed her family to be whole again. Not thinking about the germs on the floor she sits down between his legs putting her head on his thigh and takes his folded arms and places them around her.

"No more secrets Brice."

He still doesn't speak but removes the hair clip that has her hair pulled back and begins running his hands through it. She knows if it was going to work between them she must forget the past and allow them to move on together. He had to have the position as head of their family and they both knew it. She could always and did on many occasions manipulate him into doing what she wanted until she got her way, but really it had hurt her more in the end.

Somehow he'd become less important to her after the baby was born. She did what she wanted and came and went as she pleased. When he needed her the truth was she had not been there, not emotionally anyway. Yes, she was a great wife, but she treated him as though he owed her something way too often and that was wrong. Somewhere in between their troubles and triumphs she had allowed them to become lost because there was still a confused person living within her. When he spoke she listened for the first time in a long time.

"Han, I know I hurt you, but I want a chance to be your husband, a real chance. One that I don't have to compete with what I did to us each time I say something or do something. One that I don't have to complete with Connor, Miss. Ann, or even your mother. I want to be your husband and your soul mate; not Mr. Hannah Renee Chandler, but your man, your lover, and your friend."

Hearing the unrefined emotion in his voice she lifts her head and looks long and hard at his face. His eyes reflected sorrow like she'd never seen in them before. "That's what I want Brice."

Immediately he took courage. "Can you love me beyond the infidelity and not standing up and being a man like I should have from the beginning?"

"Brice you are a man, you have always been a man."

"No. I thought just getting you to marry me, paying the bills, and being a good father was all a husband was required to do. I was wrong. I was also untruthful to you and myself when I said some things didn't matter."

"Like what Brice?"

"Like when you shut me out. Han, I just can't take that. It is not that I am trying to get into your head. I just need to know if I can't fix it for you I can at least listen to you. When you shut me out like that I think you don't love me anymore or you are planning to run again and it makes my heart bleed."

"Oh Brice, I don't know what to do myself too much of the time. When I hurt or if I'm scared I shut down. When I was small it was the only way to protect myself to prevent myself from going crazy or doing something irrational. I've never had anyone love me the way you do and sometimes I am so scared you are going to leave or worse find someone to replace me. I guess I was just waiting for the day it would happen, and it did."

"I never planned on cheating Han. I could never imagine ever being with someone other than you. At first it was just an e-mail or two, then for a long time we text back and forward. When she started sending me pictures it was around the same time you seemed uninterested in us and I used that as an excuse. I know everything I should have done and could have done and I have questioned my actions a million times. You were the dream girl for me Han. Guys like me don't have women like you; except they are trophy wives and you know I am not stacked like that. I went from being in amazement to believing I could have who I wanted, but how wrong I was. I already had everything I wanted, at least sometimes anyway. Sometimes I wondered if you felt the same way. You kept our home spotless, you prepared all these gourmet meals, and you dressed and looked hot every day, but I came to believe you were just going through the motions. Maybe you missed your old life when you went off to yourself. Perhaps you regretted marrying me or even allowing me to be Joy's father, especially when you repeatedly asked about taking her to see Connor. I wondered if it was you that needed to see him."

"Connor… Brice? How could you think I wanted him? I loved you when I was with Connor. Sure I pretended to go on, but there were times I cried for you and only you. I just learned how to hide it well. The only reason I ran in the first place was because I was afraid and then your mother treated me like Miss. Ann did and I just couldn't imagine living like that again.

"I know you and my mother have issues still and I will not, I promise you, look the other way about it anymore. Will you please do something for me?"

"What is it Brice?"

"Even if I disappoint you tell me; talk to me. Up until the last year we have always had great communication and I miss that. Tell me that I am good even if I am bad every now and then. Sometimes I just need to hear that you see me beyond my faults. Unbeknownst to me but I believe you when you tell me I can do anything. Just like I believe you when you tell me I am worthless and you can't stand the sight of me."

"But you are good man Brice, that's why I came back to you. That's why for a year after I left after college I waited for you to come, to call, my heart longed for you."

"You don't say it and I thought that it was because you didn't want us. That you only stayed because of our daughter."

"I told you from the beginning I was messed up Brice. I am still working through so many things. Every time I think I am well on my way something else blindsides me and it starts all over again. You are the one that needs to decide if you are committed to staying because I know I still have some hurdles to conquer. In some areas of my life I am still screwed up and I know it."

"Oh baby, you are not, don't you see. You just have to learn to trust again. My cheating didn't help that matter I know. We just have to learn to communicate more. People that haven't been through half the things you have overcome still have communication issues. You are beautiful Han, inside and outside and I love you with all my heart. I need you too. Despite all that has happened to you, to us, I know we were meant to be together."

He pulls her up from the floor and looks at the woman he'd kill for and again says, "I love you Han. Please forgive me for what I have done to us. From this day forward I vow to be a better husband. I vow to talk to you, and when you try to shut down on me I will not allow it. Even if you become angry, I will not allow anything to come between us again. Not the past and not people. Be my wife again. Give me your heart again and I promise never to break it."

Reaching into his pocket he pulls out a ring. Being the woman she was her vanity was certain the diamond must have been at least two carets; sterling silver, flawless and breath taking. Her eyes widened. He didn't miss that moment of taking her breath away and prayed for more opportunities in their future to make her happy.

"What are you doing Brice? I have a ring and I love it."

"Yes, you do, but I want to start over and I want this to serve as a reminder that I pledged my love to you all over again. I don't want divorce to be an option for us ever again. I pray I never give you a reason to consider it. Every time you look at your hand I want you to remember this day and push harder when you want to stop or give up. Please, accept my hand in marriage again and be my wife, my friend, and lover once more, please Mrs. Chandler."

After placing the ring on her right hand he kissed her. At first slow and subtle knowing she would want more, and then firm and passionately until they are both burning with desire. Desire that could in no way be quenched on the veranda of a hotel with a napping baby just inside. At least that was what he thought until she takes his hand and slips inside. Both of them look towards the bed where their sleeping daughter lay still exhausted from her adventurous morning. She had plans for him and nothing was going to prevent her from consummating the new commitment they had made to each other just minutes earlier.

Opening the bathroom door she leads him inside locking it behind her. That was when she kissed him like she had not done before. It takes her little time at all to undress him and get down to pleasuring him. The vanity set was the perfect height for her to use as a prop for her apologetic husband. He needed to be shown he was forgiven and she was ready to be Mrs. Chandler without reservation. He'd always known his wife was an extraordinary woman. By the time they finished she'd proved herself once again and he was one exhausted happy man.

Chapter 21

It was the ringing phone that startled Hannah from a peaceful sleep. Reaching across her husband who was awake, she attempted to retrieve her mobile phone from the night stand; he prevented her. When their eyes meet, hers questioning and his sincere, she was taken back when he removed the phone from her hand and silenced the ringer and placed it back on the table. A pouty Hannah attempts to excuse herself to the restroom but her husband grabs the tail of the bathrobe she was wearing and she stopped in her tracks. Turning she faced him head-on and meets the new love of her life.

"Please baby, just us this weekend. Everything I need and want is right here in this room and right now all I need is you and I will do anything to have you." His voice was begging and his eyes pleaded with her. Her eyes mist as she realized that God truly was giving her just want she wanted for the weekend; her family and a new beginning. Overcome with emotion she says, "I love you Brice" just before the tears fall. He kisses her tears, then her neck, and finally her mouth. Locking in a French kiss that kindles the embers from their previous love making and the flame ignites. Then those same three words float into the air "I love you too daddy!" and just like that the fire is extinguished. They weren't the only ones the phone had awakened.

"Daddy I hungry!"

"I am hungry Joy, say I am hungry okay?" her mother corrects. Drying her tears she greets her daughter, "Good Afternoon my little Joy."

Joy has one thing on her mind. "I am hungry" she repeats obeying her mother but running straight to her father.

"Well let's get you dressed so we can get my little princess some food then." Kissing his wife one more time he grabs his daughter by the hand and heads for the restroom. How is my princess this afternoon? Did you nap well?"

"I hungry Daddy!"

"How does a turkey sandwich, sun chips, and an apple sound to my little Joy?"

"Dewish Daddy! Dewishes!!"

Daddy and daughter washed their hands at the sink. Hannah decided to give them bonding time and took the opportunity to shower and dress. When she emerged from the bathroom the pair were having a picnic on the floor sitting on the special blanket Johanna made for Joy's first birthday. She noticed the remaining items left in the basket: Cheese, crackers, fruit, and a bottle of non-alcoholic champagne.

Seeing her emerge from the restroom he looked away from his daughter for a minute. The gaze told her he or they rather had plans for later and Mrs. Chandler looked forward to it. For the first time in their marriage she was ready for the two of them to go away together, alone. He was a good man and she was happy he belonged to her. The truth was, after it was all said and done she still loved her husband and really wanted to spend forever with him.

Somewhere across town according to the clerk at The Chalet, there was a magic show and Brice just had to take his little princess to see it. After becoming lost once or twice, fighting with traffic and then playing cat and mouse for parking they were finally seated and ready to watch the great Master of Mystery. Joy laughed at everything from the rabbit being pulled from the hat to the card tricks, all while sitting on her father's lap. The happy couple touched one another for any reason at all, stole kisses, and held hands whenever possible. Being in love was wonderful. This time more so because it was no longer the fantasy of love that infatuated her with a bunch of feelings, but the decision to be committed that provoked the heart to engage again.

It wasn't that Hannah had ever stopped loving her husband; the pain of him not loving her was all too real. The feeling that her soul was ripped apart had given new meaning to the phrase broken hearted. Her husband touching someone else, needing someone else, and being intimate with someone other than herself was the nightmare no woman wanted. The anger, the betrayal, and heartache she felt from time to time still did not, could not douse her love for the man that made her feel complete. Of all the battles in her young life marriage by far had been the most intense.

During the course of the next hour when he wasn't stealing glances at her or she him the two enjoyed the glee on their daughter's face while she was being entertained. True to her nature Hannah people watched by scanning through the crowd of people. The city of Austin had its own salad bowl and they had come out in droves that Saturday morning. The room was filled with people, people, and more people. Some stood along the walls of the auditorium with children of all ages. People laughed, clapped, ate, squatted, and squealed. Many dressed down, some up, and others in complete cowboy attire. Small groups and large groups even solitary people groups. Babies, school age and even middle aged people with 2.5 children. She was happy their family had come.

After the magic show was over, Hannah trying to make sure that they left nothing behind was almost startled when a middle aged Caucasian woman appears at her side. "Excuse me. I just had to tell you, you have such a beautiful family. Your daughter is gorgeous."

That's all she got out before a gentleman joined her with three small children and whisks her off. Waving to her, Brice says, "Thank you Ms., and so do you." Hannah said nothing, but stored the incident in her later compartment.

After the show they take a walk downtown Austin. Hannah loved the atmosphere, the scenery, even the smell. Feeling like she was in a novel walking on the cobblestone streets peering in the shops she took it all it. She admired the lovely hanging flower baskets outside some of the stores. Smelling the food from the eateries was intoxicating. The churned ice cream, the smell of fresh pumpkin pie, the freshly popped corn, and good ole fashioned southern fried chicken was about all any of them could stand. When Brice suggested they eat by the river at one of the café's no one objected. In that moment life was perfect.

During their late dinner they talked at the family table for the first time in months. Hannah noticed the countenance of her daughter was so much better. For some reason when they were at odds it triggered her allergies or nightmares. She often went between the two of them at home because they were often in different rooms; Hannah's choice of course. When it was dinner time both she and Joy ate together and Brice alone or father and daughter shared the meal and Hannah excused herself. That was all in the past for the Chandler family. That was what she silently prayed.

Not wanting to return to the hotel room just yet the family drives around the city. When Hannah reached over and grabbed her husband's hand she must have surprised him a bit. She just needed to touch him to make sure she wasn't dreaming. He'd switched on some instrumental jazz and the ambience was perfect. She was regretting the trip back home already. She longed for more time away but found consolation in knowing she would not wait so long to plan another trip.

By the time they arrived at The Chalet Joy was fast asleep. The weather was unusually warm so Brice opened the sun roof and the two sat holding hands for a while. She knows she must tell him the other news but was petrified. The day had been perfect and she had not lived many of those so she puts it off one more day.

"Kiss me Brice." He obeys her command and kisses her for a very long time. Long enough to tell her you are the only woman for me. Hard enough to tell her I know what you need and I am pleased to give it to you. There under the Texas stars the two make out until going inside was their only option.

Without saying a word the two prepare their daughter for bed. Hannah puts her in pajamas and while her father administers her breathing treatment she decided it was the night for the peekaboo teddy and the edible undies. She was feeling really naughty and they both liked naughty. After massaging her body with his favorite fragrance she is careful to put her hair just the way he loved to see it; she emerged from the powder room with a miniature robe on. Making sure the coast was clear she positioned herself against the wall opposite where their daughter lay sleeping. One leg on the wall she allows the robe to shimmy to the floor and beckoned him to come. He immediately salutes her and takes command. God did she love when he was in control. Her body obeyed his every order. He doesn't tell her he knows something is bothering her; he just gives her what she wants until the early morning hours. Exhausted they both fall into a satisfied sleep.

When day light begins to creep into their room she was at last ready to release her secret with the fleeting darkness. She whispers, "Brice."

Immediately he answers, "Yes Baby."

"I have to tell you something." She feels a lump in her throat and attempts to swallow. He is watching her, searching. Usually those words were the beginning of a painful conversation and his concern was evident. Hannah was trying to figure out just where to begin saying words that she had not been able to speak out loud. Not even to God. There is a pregnant pause. He becomes anxious.

"What is it Baby?"

That's when the tears came. Slow at first like the snowflakes that trickle down from the mountain top just before the avalanche that buries the unsuspecting skiers and zaps their oxygen supply. Alarmed at the sorrow he sees in her face he desires to comfort her, but doesn't know if it is appropriate. He fears she planned the trip to ask for a divorce or to tell him she was leaving again. Maybe she loved the doctor in Virginia. He stares on like a deer paralyzed by the head lights of an oncoming vehicle knowing he should do something, but cannot. Reason eventually gives him a swift kick in the derriere and he decides it doesn't matter what she was about to confess he still must be a husband to his hurting wife. He had abandoned her once and he swore he would never do it again, no matter the circumstances.

"Just tell me baby…we can get through it, just say it." Drawing her too him, he is thankful that their daughter was having a sound sleep in the next bed. Sitting with his back to the headboard of the bed with her lying next to him like a worn rag doll he waits. She always talked to him when he waited.

After the morning sunrays slipped through the sheered white curtains and danced on the burgundy carpet, the birds sang their salutation to the new day, and the trees began to wake up, she found her courage.

"I'm barren Brice. The doctor said that I will never be able to have another baby."

So that's what it was he thought. The thing that made her cry often and fight more. That made her sad and withdrawn, even from their daughter at times. Why she had been drinking and thought she was covering it up, but he knew. Hating to admit it, he was happy it had not been worse. He understood her pain and secretly begged God to allow him to carry it for her. First his infidelity, then the miscarriage, and now the hope that they would have a house filled with children was demolished. He understood it all now. He cried. Mostly for her and the things that had been inflicted upon her by the people she had dared to love and trust, he was included in that number. He was hurt by the news, but was grateful for the baby he had laying in the next bed. Most people did not have what he did and it had taken losing them to realize that.

"I know it hurts Han and that is normal and may be normal for a while. But I think the best medicine for this is being thankful for the miracle we received when God gave us Joy."

Sitting up she looks a little cantankerous at her husband. "You mean it doesn't bother you that you won't ever have a child of your own?"

Now he was cross and says, "I do have a child of my own Hannah and her name is Summer Anna-Joy Chandler and I thank God for sending her to me each day."

Getting up from the bed, wearing only the designer pajama bottoms his mother purchased for his birthday, he aimlessly stares out the window. Looking on she doesn't know if he is the hero or the villain in this chapter of her life story until Joy stirs, has a coughing spell and he immediately goes to her and consoles her. Opening her eyes she sees it is her father and her eyes twinkle with joy as she says, "Daddy! Oh Daddy, I so love you daddy. You are my bestest friend." He tells his daughter, "I love you more than life itself my sweet little angel" and gives her a kiss on the mouth and proceeds to rock her back to sleep. With her head on his shoulder, his hand caressing her back, their eyes meet across the room. He blows her a kiss. A tear trickles down her face. He smiles.

Chapter 22

The drive back to San Antonio was rather short. Hannah was a little lighter but had just one more thing to tell her doting husband. Just before entering the city limits she figured was as good a time as any. Taking a deep breath she blurts out, "I must go and visit my mother Brice."

"Sounds good to me. Do you want to drop by on the way home or should we unpack and then drive over?"

When she gives him a strange look he doesn't know what to make of it. "No I have to see my birth mother, Angela. I need to find her."

It took everything for Brice to keep the car steady on the road. Shock seized him momentarily and he wondered if his bride had suddenly taken ill. Feeling the shifting of the car had shocked Hannah and Joy. The little princess wakes from her nap and scolds her father, "Careful Daddy!" and instantly slumbers again.

"Maybe I shouldn't have sprung that on you like that huh?" This time she wasn't concocting anything to break the news. The truth, just as she had promised was what she planned on telling him.

"You think" he half grinned.

For the next thirty minutes she shares with him her hospital experience, the drinking and how God had interrupted her drunken binges and finally the dream at the spa. Sitting in the driveway of their home Brice listened intently to his wife. Careful not to interject he reassured her that she had his utmost attention by removing his seatbelt and turning to face her. He was amazed by her willingness to pour her heart out to him and even more baffled that she permitted him to hear such intimate details. All he could think of was how much he loved her and repeatedly resisted the urge to grab her and kiss her because maybe that would have been rude. At least that was what his head told him, but his heart said something else and he obeyed.

The kiss, soft and reassuring made his wife throw her arms around his neck and hold him as tight as possible. To him it was a kiss, to her it said I have your support and I am not judging you nor your past actions. We are in this thing together. "I love you Brice!" She just couldn't help herself.

"Oh baby, baby, baby!" He belts out and then begins to sing, "You are my sunshine, my only sunshine. You make me happy cause I have you!"

Laughing she argues, "That isn't how the song goes Ant!"

"Oh but it is…that's the Chandler version."

She laughs and his heart does a somersault just thinking about the miracle of a new beginning with the woman he loved. Hearing her call him by the pet name she'd given him was like pouring liquid joy to his soul. Seeing her laughing and being genuinely happy was living proof that there was a God that cared about them both.

Unpacking didn't take long and neither did preparing the late lunch. Hannah busied herself preparing steaks for the grill, the potatoes were in the oven and Brice tossed the salad. Joy was walking through the house talking on her toy phone to Johanna and every time she turned her back her parents were at it again. In the closet, in the laundry room, and even in the room she had learned to hate so much. She refused to give another woman her house and she vowed to make their place home again.

Later that afternoon they visited Johanna. She was feeling a little under the weather and Hannah wanted to take care of her mother for a change. She knew that things had been strained between them and that was a Hannah issue, not a Johanna issue. Johanna Hemley's heart's desire was to take care of her family and she had put her children's needs above everything, except God. She had not thought twice about giving up her life in Washington, her lifelong friends, and her church to be with the daughter she says God sent her. Yet each time that same daughter went through something painful, once again she pushed her away in some degree or another.

When Hannah let herself in with her personal keys there was no sign of her mother. That worried Hannah and Brice knew it. Quickly moving ahead of her he calls out, "Mom, it's me, Brice, I'm coming back there."

That was her warning call to take cover if need be. Just in case he did not want his wife getting there first and see something she could not handle. Knocking on the bedroom door he slowly pushed it open but she was not there. She hadn't been in the kitchen, in her favorite chair, or in the sunroom. Feeling his wife's trepidations he prays in his heart for her to be alright. When he remembered there was only one other place she could be, he almost sprints to her prayer room. Certain that was the only answer he was flabbergasted when that room was also empty.

Close to tears a worried Hannah who was hot on his trail asks to know one in particular, "Where could she be?"

"Now baby don't get yourself upset. I'm sure there is a logical explanation."

"What explanation? Her car is in the driveway and she isn't here. How could she just vanish? She doesn't have her cell phone and you know she never leaves home without that phone or her Bible." Her voice is noticeably trembling now and her anxiousness made little Joy nervous.

Brice picks up his daughter and leads his wife over to the sofa to sit down. "I'm going to look around outside, just stay here and try not to worry. I am sure she is just fine." Trying to distract their daughter he switches on the television to one of the shows she liked to watch. Hannah doesn't respond either way. The nervous wreck she felt inside had become her outward apparel. Rocking methodically she racked her brain to see if her mother had mentioned anything earlier in the day when she spoke with her. She comes up empty. After several minutes of doing nothing Hannah is about ready to pick up the phone and call the police when the door swings open. She doesn't want to face her husband of which she is certain has no good news so she continues to nervously search for the number to the local police until Joy squeals, "Grandmother!" Turning on her heels Hannah drops the phone and whirls around, "Mommy!" and greets her like she did the first time she came to San Antonio for the birth of little Joy. "Oh Mommy I was so worried! I thought something happened to you or you suddenly became ill. My heart hurt when I just couldn't find you Mommy."

Johanna did not want to let her babies go, the one on her leg nor the one with the tight grip around her neck. Overcome with happiness she attempts to console Hannah. "Oh Baby Girl I didn't mean to worry you." While she was still speaking, in came the one and only Miss. Lucy.

Hannah was still very close in her mother's arms. Her head was on her shoulder and Joy tightly held her leg demanding she be picked up. Hannah kisses her mother on the cheek and says, "I promise I am going to be a better daughter. I love you Mommy."

Johanna knows something most definitely, without a doubt, unequivocally has transpired in her daughter's life and the load she had been carrying for some time suddenly lifts. Her eyes mist over and she kisses both Hannah and Joy and tells them, "I love you too Baby Girl, always."

Brice being the goofball he could be at any given time yells, "Wait a minute, let me get some of that loving."

The room erupts with laughter and Miss. Lucy comes to the rescue. "Well bless the Lord it is a family reunion!"

Brice is on a roll and can't help himself at that point. "Well let's eat then. Can't have a reunion without having plenty of good food and I am famished!"

"Brice!" Hannah scolds. "You are always hungry."

Coming to his rescue Johanna argues, "Leave my son alone. You know I can prepare a meal in less than thirty minutes because I have it like that." Snapping her fingers she heads to the kitchen. "What do you want my precious son?"

Hannah speaks for her husband. "Now Mommy you haven't been feeling well. Don't you dare go in that kitchen to make anything for us. I came by, WE came by to check on you." With that she gives her husband a pretentious evil eye. "Do you want me to make chicken soup for you?"

"Chicken soup my dear is for sick people and that I am not."

"But Mommy when I spoke to you this morning you sounded terrible." A concerned Hannah was confused.

"Baby Girl you have got to learn to stay out of God's business. Now go sit down and let me do what I do."

Pots were already rattling, water running, vegetables sizzling, and just as promised in twenty-eight minutes they all sat around the dinner table. They feast on southern fried chicken, rice pilaf, broccoli and cheese, and her famous corn bread dressing. For a while there is a silent recitation.

Even Joy acted as though she hadn't been fed that day. She sits next to her grandmother swinging her feet and humming while she devours her rice. The pilaf was by far her favorite. Johanna had a special way of making her eat things she swore were yuck by adding them in very small pieces to the dishes. She fooled her every time. Between helpings Brice came up for air long enough to wink at his wife or play footsies with her under the table. Miss. Lucy was the first to officially speak and it was a blow to Hannah.

"What are you going to name that little baby?" Smiling, Hannah tries to hide the dagger she felt in her heart. Maybe Miss. Lucy didn't remember that she'd had a miscarriage a few months earlier. Searching for words to say her husband comes to her rescue.

"Miss. Lucy we have decided to stick with the one. Our little princess is just enough for us to handle."

Johanna looks on a bit confused by the conversation but more concerned because her son-in-law was speaking for her daughter. Especially when she knew that it was her heart's desire to have more children.

"Well you better get ready because whether you want it or not you will have another child. I don't know when but you will." Miss. Lucy was as sure of herself as the rain in Seattle. Getting up she said her goodbyes and proceeded to make her exit, but then turned with something else to say. "You win. Remember that. God told me to tell you, you win and to hold on to what He said because you are going to need it." With that she gave her prized hugs and off she went with her bangle bracelets and gardenia perfume.

Neither Hannah nor Brice had a clue as to what the last statement meant but as Jane's grandmother always said, "Time will tell" so she let it go. No one knew about the secret of not being able to conceive but Hannah, her husband, the doctor, and God. Perhaps God had remained silent about the issue just like she had for so long and Miss. Lucy just got it all wrong. Hannah quickly excused herself to start the dishes and anyone looking on would have missed the pain in her eyes, but not her husband and certainly not her mother.

After walking her church friend to the door Johanna joins Brice and Hannah in the kitchen. The pair was still standing at the sink washing dishes without saying anything to each other. For a minute she stood in the doorway and looked on. Two things were evident; they were undeniably in love and they had a secret.

Announcing, "Let me finish the clean-up and you two go have a seat" she hoped to give them the time they needed with one another.

"It is the least we can do after having you get off your bed of affliction to feed the hungry" Brice teased. "Why don't you go create some special moments with that granddaughter of yours that thinks the world of you? We're almost done anyway."

Believing it to be a diversion Johanna takes his advice and she and Joy head to the back yard. Joy was delighted. When the door closed behind them he takes his wife in his arms.

"Hannah Renee Chandler I love you with all my heart. Do not do this to yourself. All I ever wanted was you and wow, God gave me so much more. Please don't be sad baby. We, especially you, have spent enough time in sorrow, let's not lose the happiness we've been given."

She closes her eyes, and does her best to shake off the sudden sadness. By the time he finishes rubbing her back and encouraging her, she has made up her mind that she would not be sad each time she sees a baby. Nor will she wear her heart on her sleeve when asked about adding to their family. They were a young couple and the subject was sure to come up periodically. She concluded after that incident she would know how to handle the subject the next time and hold on to her peace at the same time.

"Ant."

"Yes Baby."

"Do you think I should tell Mommy?"

"If it were Joy would you want her to keep it from you?"

"I would be devastated if she did something like that? I want to be there for my daughter in good times and in the not so good times."

"Then there is your answer."

"I love you Mr. Chandler. More than you will ever know."

"Oh I plan on finding out over the next seventy-five years."

"Ummm," is all she says and stays right where he'd pulled her into the comfort and safety of his arms. She didn't know if it was the lack of love shown to her in those important adolescent and teenage years, but there was something absolutely soothing and comforting about being held by him. He didn't attempt to push her away or hurry her through her healing but allowed her to take as much time as she needed. Maybe that was why she had fallen so madly in love with him. She could always count on his touch and his ears. He'd kept her secrets all through college and he still kept them now; the abortion being the only exception. She guessed even men needed a shoulder to cry on every now and then.

When she lifted her head it was with reluctance, but she knew the longer they stayed inside, the more her mother was bound to become suspicious. "Guess it's confession time."

"Not until you're ready Han. Take your time and tell her when you're ready, okay."

She agreed and they both walk outside together just in time to hear Joy telling her grandmother about their weekend trip. "…And Grandmother hes pulled a burd from hes hat and it fly away and daddy gave me candy, it was blue. Then daddy kiss Mommy too, alots."

"Wow! Sounds like you had a great deal of fun princess." Johanna seems thoroughly interested in everything her granddaughter has to say.

Brice whispers in his wife's ear, "She's enough" and Hannah's heart smiles in total agreement.

When Joy sees them she squeals, Daddy…Mommy! I so missed you!" As usual he picks her up and swirls her around and says, "And daddy so missed you too Princess Joy."

Hannah takes a seat in one of the lawn chairs next to her mother. Brice grabs a ball and starts a game with his daughter. Johanna seizes this perfect opportunity to have a little chat with her one and only daughter.

"You okay Baby Girl?"

"Mommy I don't know when I've been better to tell you the truth. This weekend was great Mommy; just what we needed. We're going to make it. My family is going to be just fine."

"You don't know how that filled my heart with happiness baby. A blind person could feel how in love you two are. Plus I almost grabbed my sunglasses because of the ring on your finger."

Excited Hannah waves her hand in the air showing the two caret diamond off. "Isn't it beautiful?"

Brice pretends not to see her display. The man in him sticks his chest out a little further, then he remembers only God could have brought them as far as they'd come and says an audible "Thank you."

"Mommy I have to tell you something really important but it's difficult to say."

"Just say it Baby Girl. When you finish speaking you will still be my daughter just like you are now. So shoot."

Just as she had shared with her husband in detail, she tells her mother about the dreams, drinking, and the conversation with God about Ms. Ann. Johanna listens intently and then says, "That is awesome baby. Making peace with your past and forgiving is the only way to have a future." Without notice tears begin to stream down her face and she says, "My baby has grown up on me, my God."

"Oh Mommy, thank you for not giving up on me." Now it is time for the daughter to wipe her mother's tears away; perhaps for the very first time.

They spend a little more time visiting and then make their exit. Brice has Joy in his arms and a plate of food for later and lunch the next day. Hannah shakes her head but can't really blame him, her mother was a chef connoisseur and everyone knew it. On the drive home her husband announced, "Tomorrow we begin our search for your birth mother." She did not argue. It was time they put this last thing behind them and got on with the rest of their lives.

Chapter 23

The search for Miss. Ann was not as simply as anyone of them thought it would be. From all appearances she had dropped off the face of the earth. Every lead she'd given the detective was a dead end. Her home had tenants who knew not of her whereabouts. The pastor of the church she'd attended for all those years had a bout of amnesia. The neighbors would not or could not say anything to the private detective they had hired. After that first week Hannah and Brice knew something did not smell right.

By the beginning of the following week Hannah knew she was going to have to drive back to the place she'd sworn to never return; Kristina, Florida. With Thanksgiving only four days away she knew she would have to wait until after the holiday before taking the journey of all journeys. Her mind wandered often about her birth mother's whereabouts. Unfortunately, that wasn't all that weighed heavy on her. Things had been going so well she just didn't want to be the one to put mud in the water, but she was dreading spending one minute with China Chandler. Having vowed to be honest in their marriage she knew she must, if just for her peace of mind bring up the subject. So one night after a hot make out session she told her husband how she felt.

"Brice, must we go to your mother's for Thanksgiving? I just don't want to go."

He says nothing. She wonders why but doesn't ask. After several minutes pass he speaks into the darkness. "That's just it Han. It isn't just my mother's house. It is my parents' home and I would like to see them and my brothers and sisters who will be there for the first time this year. I'll protect you." With that he kisses her and rolls over and falls asleep. At least that's what she thinks. She lay awake for a while dreading Thanksgiving at the Chandler's house then eventually attempts to cry herself to sleep. A quiet cry that only God could interpret. She was careful not to allow one tear to fall but somehow he knew and after about an hour turns the light on and sits up in the bed. She doesn't move but lay staring at the wall.

"Come here."

"No Brice, I just want to go to sleep. You have work in the morning and I have stuff so a good night's rest will do us both good." She doesn't want to argue. Nor does she want family discussions in their bedroom and instantly regrets bringing up the subject.

"Come here Han." His voice was commanding, yet gentle. She couldn't deny him either way. Sitting up in the bed beside him she braced herself for a lecture. "We've been through a lot and I know I haven't always given you reason to trust me. I've let you down. I haven't covered you in the past, but this won't be one of those times. I promise. Please will you just trust me baby?"

This time she doesn't say anything. His mother was so mean at times and after the last several months of misery she'd gone through she just wanted to be around people that loved her for the holidays. He wouldn't understand that so finally she just agreed so they could both go to bed.

"Alright Brice, I'll trust you." She wasn't convincing so he let the conversation go, but not his wife. Grabbing her hand he pulls her closer to him and this time they both slept.

By the time Thanksgiving Day arrived Hannah and her pecan pie were ready to face the other Chandler's. Not because she'd had a change of heart but because each time negative thoughts came to her mind she thought about the husband she loved so much. She thought about how she felt about her mother Kimberlee and understood that sometimes a child just wants his mother and she could and would respect that. She would miss Johanna but was sure at some point before the day was done she would be able to visit her and have that peace cobbler she craved.

As they drove down the long driveway to the mini mansion Brice squeezes his wife's hand in reassurance. She was too busy eyeing the array of vehicles of the people that had already arrived. Both his sisters, Rebecca and Kayla were there but she wondered about that red headed step child she had grown to love so much and the god-father of their daughter Minister

Ian Cole. This would be their first time seeing him since their reconciliation. He'd worn out his tennis shoes traveling and was just returning from a mission's trip and Hannah could not wait to hear the juicy details. She had no idea if Nick and his wife would make an appearance. He probably would not leave his mother's side on Thanksgiving Day to be with the wicked step mother, but only time would tell.

Hannah did the sign of the cross as her husband turned the door to make their entrance and whispered before crossing the Dead Sea, "God save the queen and me too."

"Tony Bear!!!! Aww my baby is finally here. I was beginning to think you didn't love your dear sweet mother!" She chides. Kissing him on the cheek, she grabs his hand and leads him off to the waiting family. "Look whose here everyone!"

Hannah assumed in her excitement she had become blind and did not notice she and Joy standing there holding the pecan pie. It was possible that before she lead her husband astray that they had become invisible or maybe the Martians zapped them when they landed at the nuthouse. Whatever the case, Brice was not having it. He turned and grabbed his wife's hand and scoops up his beloved daughter and says, "Yes, the other Chandler's have arrived so let the party began. Hello Mother, it's good to be home" and continues to greet the remainder of his family. China Chandler who looks as though she has been slapped in the face has a quick comeback. "Peachy, my entire family is here. My girls and I are about to check on dinner. Becky, Kayla come along now." When Brice tells her to take the pie Hannah has so graciously made with them to the kitchen she pretends she has just noticed the hand that has been extended to her.

"Why thank you dear" she says and tells her husband to "Do something with that" and waltzes off making a grand exit into the gourmet kitchen with its triple ovens, stainless steel appliances and marble counter tops. Hannah breathes a sigh of relief. That is when she noticed that Nick and his wife, Megan along with their two boys were seated in the great room among the rest of the outcast of the Chandler descendants. Kayla's husband, their daughter Khloe, Rebecca's beau, and a few family friends all make small talk until they are finally summoned for dinner. Until then Hannah enjoyed the refuge she had found among Brice's half-brothers.

Hannah takes a seat next to Ian and right away he starts in on her, "Hi Curly Sue, life looks good on you."

She whispers, "You red headed step-child I've missed you bunches. Don't stay gone so long next time."

He chortles and the two of them become engrossed in conversation for the next hour or so. Brice jumps in and out between serving the guest with drinks or whatever else they required. Hannah was forbidden in the kitchen. Nick and Megan have their hands full dealing with their four month old twins Ashton and Patton. Joy was having fun playing with Kloe when she was not trying to mother the twins. The men talked much about football, football, and football while watching football and the women, well the ones that knew each other conversed and the others didn't. When the dinner bell was summoned, literally the tiny little silver bell that Lady China rang and said, "Dinner is served," everyone was ravenous.

The formal dining room looked like something out of a magazine. The décor, the setting, and the food were only the finest of the finest. All went great until the seating arrangements, and then it was all downhill from there. The elegant table had seating for twelve. Twelve people that had name cards to assure they knew just where to sit. Positioned at the head of the house of course sat Mr. and Mrs. Chandler. The two sisters and their men plus five year old Kloe all had seating at the prestigious table. Then there was room for Lady China's favorite aunt, her husband, the Chandler's two god daughters, Layla and Lauren, and then it just happened that there was only one last chair available and it was designated for Brice. How convenient. Everyone else had seating in the breakfast nook or the kitchen table and was quickly and quietly ushered to their places.

When Brice realized what was going on Hannah witnessed the vein in his head protrude and she did not want to cause a scene, especially on Thanksgiving. She considered it an honor to sit with her brothers-in-law and to her the company was far better. Putting her hand on his shoulder she whispers she would be fine and to her shock and dismay obscenity disgorge out of his mouth. That was likening to Mother Teresa in her time taking an AK47 and going on a shooting spree. She didn't know what to say or do to stop the explosion. God did. For once she witnessed Mr. Chandler step up and take charge.

"My dear we're missing a chair for Hannah. I will go and get one and we can get down to this fine meal."

Needless to say his remarks did not help the matter at all. China set the record straight with, "Well I didn't think she would come darling. Oh dear, now we have to disfigure this beautiful setting."

Tired of her antics Hannah is forthcoming. "Actually, Mrs. Chandler it would be an honor to sit with my brothers in the other room." Hannah was cagily to her monster-in-law. The house had a very spacious and open floor plan so although it was in the next room you could still see and hear pretty much everything taking place in the other rooms. Turning she adds, "You needn't bother Mr. Chandler the other room is perfect." Smiling she meant every word she'd spoken. That was not enough for the wicked witch of the west though because her reply, "Now see, look at the way things always work out. Now be a jewel and run along now so we can say grace."

Looking at his mother through the eyes of a soon be serial killer Brice's voice thunders, "Don't you go anywhere Han. Dad get the chair please."

Not one person said anything, to include China Chandler. Once Hannah was seated next to him and Joy on his lap was the only other time Brice spoke to anyone. Even then it was only to make sure his wife was comfortable. When Mr. Chandler asked Ian, who was seated in the adjacent room to do the honors and bless the food, the atmosphere lightened a bit Hannah actually sees her husband's shoulders relax. When Mr. Chandler has Nick help him carve the turkey the gesture adds to Brice's good mood, but it doesn't last long.

In keeping with the Thanksgiving tradition of the Chandler's home they go around the table and share one important blessing they are thankful to have been given within that year. Guest always start the tradition so it takes a while to get to the head table. Most say the same thing; family, life, health or something along those lines. When only the hosts are left to speak, of course Mr. Chandler allows his wife of thirty years to go first. That is when all hell unleashed on its unsuspecting pry.

Dressed in a white designer coat dress she looked fit to have dinner with the president. Her ear rings were stunning and she had the beauty that did not require make-up, although she wore lashes and lip gloss regardless. Standing to make her speech she formally welcomes each guest into her home. She was thankful for, "The man that made her the happiest woman alive thirty years ago and still today. For the beautiful children we share and…" becoming choked up and teary eyed she stops briskly fanning her eyes with perfectly manicured hands as not to disturb her make-up. Forcing herself to go on she began speaking again. "I am so very very thankful for the blessing of my sweet little granddaughter Kloe. For, for… my two little grandchildren who are now in heaven with God. The room gasp and people touch one another in curiosity. Others raise eye brows and some even whisper. There is a low, "Poor thing" heard, followed by a "My my my". Right on cue China Chandler continues, "One day my little Tony bear is going to have other children and I pray God will bless him really soon and be merciful to his wife."

Hannah felt her blood boiling inside her and unconsciously picked up the empty plate from the table ready to use it as a weapon. Surprisingly she heard a voice say, "I have this" and peace washed over her. Grateful that she could hear God even in the midst of a war zone she relaxes back into her chair. She doesn't realize it was not God at all that had spoken those words until it was too late.

"Mother from this day forward you will never have to worry about me, my wife, or my daughter coming to this house again. Never again will I subject my wife to your bigotry, self-righteousness, and pure hatred. This is my wife, whom I love with all my heart and this little angel is truly my joy. Since you cannot accept them, you lose me too, because I have had enough. You insult them, exclude them, and do everything in your power to ostracize them. Well I have news for you mother, that is not the Christian way so you had better check your status on the heavenly roll because I am really doubtful. To the rest of you, I apologize for this interruption, but to my family, I am sorry I came here today. With that he takes his wife and daughter by the hand and says "Good-bye" and does not look back.

Quarrel was an understatement to what had just taken place. Shock had pierced the atmosphere, the tears, the heartache, and the pain of those that genuinely needed the love of a real family. Leaving that way should have made Hannah happy. Her husband stood up for her, protected her just like he promised he would, but knowing his family, their family was torn did not make her feel good. She wasn't the only one it bothered she was sure. Not even Joy made a sound from her car seat in the back. She sensed something was going on with her daddy and that made her little world troubled. When Brice signaled to get off on Johanna's exit Hannah said, "No Brice, let's just go home."

"Han we are not going home without seeing Mom. Besides she has a pound cake with my name on it." He was endeavoring to be humorous but she saw the hurt in his eyes. He and Johanna had been close from the very beginning and although the affair had challenged their relationship it still came out stronger than before. Hannah knew he needed her strength, not her food. By now they were all feeling a bit starved. She was grateful she'd given Joy a sandwich before leaving home that afternoon.

When Johanna's male friend answered the door it took everything in Hannah not to display attitude. I mean really who does that? This is not his house, were just a few of her thought avalanche. Remembering the fact that they had just left world war three back at the Chandler's humbled her rather quickly.

Johanna was overjoyed to see her family come through her door so unexpectedly. Right away she analyzed the situation and immediately began to pray within herself. Pleased that she prepared a big meal despite not planning to have a lot of guest, she immediately went to the kitchen. After hygiene and grace for the next several minutes they have a real Thanksgiving dinner, in peace. They eat up everything placed on their plates. Brice has seconds, not unusual for him, but Hannah saves room for dessert. Joy falls asleep at the table. After Johanna cleans up the mash potato face and cranberry hands she attempts to place Joy in her special room at grandma's house, but her daddy says no.

"Give her to me, I'll hold her Mom." Mother and daughter exchange glances. After scooping up his baby he joins Mr. Jefferies in the living room to watch the game. The scene hurts his wife. It was one of many reasons she knew he was heartbroken. What do we do about this God was her heart's cry? The scene back at Millwood had been an open attack on her but her husband took it personally. Her abortion and her miscarriage had become public knowledge, meant to shame her, belittle her, but it had only driven a family apart. Strangely, she felt liberated. Now she knew that nothing she could ever do would make her good enough for Brice's mother. She would never be accepted by China Chandler because in her eyes she wasn't worthy of her son. Hannah finally realized that it was no longer her problem but something Mrs. China must deal with.

After she and her mother tidy up the kitchen they attempt to have some girl time, but her husband calls out, "Hey baby come sit next to me and watch the game." She complies. Feeling his pain she was committed to do everything she could to help him through his hurt. For the next several hours the women half watch the game while the men yell at the television, eat more dessert than they should have and indulge in some great conversation. With each moment they spend at her mother's home Hannah feels the heavy weight become lighter and lighter. Specifically after Brice shuts his phone off that had constantly rang since they'd left his parent's. Every chance he was given to touch her, caress her, even kiss her in front of her mother, which made her somewhat uncomfortable, he availed himself. His daughter in his right arm and his wife in his left arm was like medicine to him. It was the prescription he needed.

When Joy woke from her nap she demanded right away the slice of pie her grandmother had promised. While she sat at the breakfast bar eating ice cream and pumpkin pie Hannah at last had the opportunity to bring her mother up to speed. This recount of the day's activities brought out the mother in Johanna and she became irate. This was mostly due to the ill treatment of her daughter and granddaughter and the sadness so vivid in her son-in-law's eyes.

"Now I understand why Brice looked so defeated when he walked through the door. How are you holding up Baby Girl? The truth."

"Mommy I am fine. Sure I didn't like my business put on display like that but I refuse to hold my head down anymore. If anything it assures me that my husband and I were meant to be together. Isn't that what you always told me? That if the devil is so busy fighting you, then you must be doing something correct? I love my husband and our past is just that. I feel like we have a second chance, like I have a new heart, and I am not going to allow anyone to take that away from me."

"Good for you baby. It is affecting that my little innocent Joy was caught in the cross fire. Mistreatment of children is evil and she made sure you and everyone there knew she does not accept my little angel. Thank God she is too young to really know what is going on. At least I hope she doesn't anyway. With that little genius you can never tell."

"Oh Mommy, I'm so glad we have you. I know I am not always appreciative but I am so thankful for a mother that loves me and embraces me and my family no matter what. Brice loves you so much for just that reason I am sure of it. I thought we were going home but he insisted on coming here."

After the game was over they played some board games, ate a little more, and then play more games. Mr. Jefferies said good-night around ten and not long after they followed suit. Hannah had never been as thankful as when they pulled up to their brick house with black shudders in cul-de-sac. It had been a long day. After getting Joy settled in bed she was elated to take refuge in their bedroom and have some one on one time with the man she loved. She did not want to discuss the events that took place at his parent's so she steered clear of the subject. He would tell her when he was ready to talk.

"Brice, next year may I have Thanksgiving here? With T, Ian, Nick and their families, Mommy, Jane and RJ, and whomever you want to invite?"

She knew he was still upset about the day's events. Still very quiet since leaving his parent's home he continued to watch the television. When he remained that way for too long she walks over to where he sat in the leather chair by their bedroom window and rubbed his head.

"I am so in love with you that I never want to think about living my life without you. God sent you to me and I am so grateful. Whatever you want to do is fine with me, as long as we are together nothing else matters." Having said her peace she kisses him on the head and turns to walk to the restroom to prepare for bed. Before she reached the door he broke the silence.

"Do you really mean that?" He sounded so sad it hurt her heart to hear it.

"Yes Ant, I mean every word of it."

Nodding his head he turns back to the game he had been pretending to watch. Suddenly turning to his wife again he says, "We leave for Florida on Monday morning to find Miss. Ann."

Hannah didn't know what to say. How? When? And so many questions tapped danced through her mind. Knowing how she worked he says without turning from the television, "Jackson gave me his leave time. It's time for you to obey God. By the way Johanna is coming to help us with Joy. You know, just in case we need her."

Stunned she stood in the doorway of the restroom staring at the man she'd married that never ceased to amaze her. The husband she was finding had so many things about him she was just discovering; to include a strength that she found so attractive.

Chapter 24

When the Chandlers merged onto the interstate at three a.m. the following Monday morning they were glad to have their mother along. The trip would be sixteen hours and thirty-seven minutes too long for a two year old to be confined to a car seat. The first day they traveled until Joy became cranky. Since leaving so early in the morning she slept quite a bit until around three in the afternoon and then her sirens went off. Finding a child friendly hotel with a suite they allowed her to play on the indoor playground for as long as she could stand it. Afterwards they returned to the hotel room and ordered room service. Brice was exhausted and dosed on the couch, camouflaging it as resting his eyes. After his own snoring woke him he admitted he was beat and off to bed he went. Hannah had no such luck. Question after question slammed into Hannah's soul like hurricane winds. She longed to wake her husband to talk but knew she had better speak to the one who was sending her back to the past in the first place.

What would she say to the woman she'd spent most of her life hating? "God sent me to tell you I forgive you?" How do you begin a conversation with a person you never wanted to speak to again, let alone see? Johanna was in prayer mode and retired to her bedroom. Joy was content to be out of the car and sat next to her mother on the couch playing with her dolls.

Around midnight, exhausted from worrying, Hannah took a sleeping Joy to her mother's bedroom and climbed in bed next to her husband. His censors went off and he opened his eyes. "Where is my baby?"

"With Mommy, I needed to be with you tonight Brice."

More awake now, he sat up and with concern in his voice he said, "Talk to me Baby."

She becomes emotional. No words could describe how she felt. Fear of the unknown gripped her like a hostage and she was unable to free herself.

"Have I told you lately how proud I am of you? You are the strongest woman I have ever had the pleasure of meeting." As he speaks she puts her head on his lap and closes her eyes and just listens. "Forget about all those what ifs of doubt that are coursing through your mind. The only thing you need to ponder is what if God does exactly what He said He would. Baby He won't lead you into failure; remember that."

Still feeling the waves of the winds of her terror storm she thrust out, "May we pray together like we used to Ant?"

"That is the perfect thing to do right now Han."

What he told God she was oblivious to because by the time he said amen she was already fast asleep. She didn't think God would mind anyway. After all, what he told God about her, about them, was between him and God. She just needed peace for her soul and that had come as soon as he had completed the first sentence, "Lord I come to you on behalf of my sweet wife…" That was enough for her.

Around five o'clock the next morning her eyes opened to peace and joy. Smiling in the darkness she thanked God because she knew He was responsible. You could not get what she felt in a bottle or from a pillow. Rolling over she massages her husband's chest, then kisses him like it was the last time she would ever see him. His libido woke up before he did. Glad they knew Johanna slept with the scriptures playing they broke in the hotel bed. Tapping out a soft rhythm on the mattress, while their bodies made music to the drone of the headboard, all was left to do was the singing. Hannah provided that with her moans and groans, while her husband answered every plea. She wanted to scream in ecstasy, she needed to scream and he knew it. Kissing her in the way that would make the French blush he stifled her cries of pleasure and the two held on to each other as they both enter into the promise land together. Her gripping his chocolate body leaving marks on his back and him with both hands full of her hair.

He breathed out, "Now that's a wakeup call! I have to work out more woman you almost killed me."

Playfully she says, "You would have died a happy man."

"Oh yeah! I have to take you to a hotel more often girl. You have a lot of nasty in you."

"You loved every bit of it."

"You got that right and don't you forget it. You are the best thing that has every happened to me Baby. God gave me my good thing just like that Bible says. You are my virtuous woman."

"Now what makes me think you really mean that Mr. Chandler?"

"Because I really do. You bring out things in me I never had knowledge I possessed."

With that the two lay in bed for another hour just holding each other and talking. They'd meant to get started at six, but it was well after seven before they have breakfast and become a part of the morning traffic. No one was bothered by the change in plans; least of all the happy couple. The atmosphere was lighter. Joy was content and Johanna was singing or humming some tune much of the trip.

When they pulled into Kristina around eleven that morning Hannah knew precisely where to go. The church on the hill where they said, "Everybody was welcome." She didn't understand what everybody meant apparently because the only people she ever saw them embrace where the ones with money, an extra honey, and the ones that acted a lot funny. It was the only place she was aware of that you could sit on the same row with your wife and your girlfriend. Where Bubba and is lover sang in the choir together, and you could usher in daisy dukes. Of course that was Monday through Saturday. Sunday was different. On Sunday you wore your best because that was the only day of the week God made visitations at Jubilee Tabernacle. Even then He only visited certain privileged people it appeared. Like Ms. Brant who when His holiness moved upon her she just could not keep it to herself, oh no. She waltzed up to the front of the church screaming, "He's on me church! I got Him." Hannah had never been sure what she had but she was certain Ms. Brant could get a check from the state for having it.

Then there was Mr. Sands who just happened to be crippled until "It" got him and then he was able to run leaps and bounds in a single service.

Unfortunately, it never stayed long because before the preacher got up he and his cane had to be helped to a seat and down to the disability office every month to assure his benefits continued to come. Oh and Mrs. Clara was a favorite. Loved everybody, throwing kisses and giving hugs but never could stand when she felt her soul stirring. Her husband caught her every Sunday, such a good man, before she hit the floor and stained her beautiful cloths. Until he fell asleep one Sunday and she caught a fainting spell and fell on Sister Mary's baby who was sitting in her carrier behind them. After Sister Mary slapped her she never caught the spirit again. After all the baby was the miracle that Sister Mary had prayed for and one day after fifteen years she'd finally come. Everyone knew it wasn't a miracle that had sent her, but her best friend's husband. How nice of her to make them the baby's god-parents and all. No one ever had the heart to tell her husband that his soldiers had never learned to swim. He'd died thinking he was the man. Sad he wasn't the only man sleeping in his bed; just one of many.

The memories of Jubilee Tabernacle all came flooding back as she pulled into the parking lot of the old white building with the cemetery in the back. The parking lot was still gravel. She guessed the building fund was still working on their fund raisers so it could be completed. Somebody should have informed them that Mr. Carter's barbeque and Ms. Bonnie's pies just wasn't going to do the job. They served their purpose though, if you needed a good laxative or a quick weight lost method.

True to his habits, the Reverend Marshall Law was sitting at his desk when Hannah stepped through the doors of the church office. Mrs. Kennedy, his secretary, was nowhere to be found. He obviously did not know that because he never looked up from his desk until Hannah stood in the opened doorway of his office. When she says, "Excuse me" she was sure she was going to have to make good use of her recent CPR training. He displayed all the signs of a person having a heart attack. When he grabbed the medication bottle and threw some pills into his mouth she wondered if she should be nervous herself.

Apologetically Hannah tells him, "I'm sorry, it wasn't my attention to startle you."

After pulling himself together he motions for her to come in and have a seat. Regaining his composure he replies, Oh child it's quite alright. My my Hannah Renee it has been a mighty long time since Kristina has seen or heard from you. To what do I owe this unexpected visit?"

On the tip of her tongue was "I am not a child, as a matter for your information, I don't think I've ever been a child" but the moment passes. "Well, I was hoping you might be of some assistance to me. I am trying to find Miss. Ann."

"It has been a minute since I've seen her in services myself Miss. Hannah."

Something in her said she was dealing with a lying preacher, but she was not giving up. "I've traveled a long way to see her and any information you may have to aid me would be most appreciated."

"Is that right? Where do you call home now Miss. Hannah?"

Again her smart mouth wanted to say none of your business, but she says, "Texas."

"Wow, Texas. Now that is a hot place, but I heard it was nice. Me, I never got around to heading west. Maybe one day before I die. Who knows what the good Lord has in store for me before I leave this place."

By then Hannah was clinching her teeth. Florida at times felt as close to hell as she ever planned on getting. You could pretty much expect it to be hot on any given Holiday and he was talking about Texas. Attempting to remain focused she steered the subject back to Miss. Ann.

"Her home has tenants and they have no idea how to reach her. I was really hoping you could help me Reverend Marshall."

"Wish I could, but like I said earlier, she has not been in the services lately. Sorry Miss. Hannah, wish I could help more."

No surprise, he was not going to help her and any further time spent in his presence was wasting precious time. It was Tuesday and they only had until Friday. Turning on her heels to leave she says, "Thank you Reverend Marshall. I'll let myself out" and was gone. She had a plan B, and so she put it into action before driving from the church parking lot.

She was certain one person would know precisely where she was and he would tell her even if she had to threaten him. Good old deacon booty call. Others knew him as Deacon Frank but she had a whole lot more knowledge of him than even his wife did.

Having been forced to go to their home whenever she was allowed to venture out of her prison cell, Hannah had no problem remembering which house was the Frank's. Miss. Ann thought maybe if she got her to fall for the deacon's son she would be able to lure him away from his wife. Wrong answer. Leroy was as much a scrub as the end of a mop. So not her type she could not even stand the sight of him let alone his big crusty lips coming into contact with her skin. Not to mention he was as dumb as a bucket of rocks.

When Mrs. Frank answered the door she was genuinely surprised and happy to see Hannah. She had been one of the few decent people at Jubilee Tabernacle.

"Oh my word! If it isn't little Hannah Renee all grown up! Hugging her she immediately invited her in and offered her tea.

"No Ma'am, no tea but I would love to talk with you though? How's the family?"

Lighting a cigarette she starts talking a mile a minute. "Baby as well as can be expected. You know me and Arthur always had a problem and it ain't getting no better. Sometimes these ole knees just won't take me where I want to go. I swear foe God my daddy was the tin man. My old man around her somewhere. I guess he making it, hard to tell if he living or dying some days. But I guess he still living cause I ain't got that insurance check!" Laughing abruptly she slaps Hannah on the back and continues to talk. She doesn't notice that she has knocked the wind out of her. "Leroy, you remember my son Leroy. He always was sweet on you, well he's dating now. Yup, finally got himself a girlfriend. I'm sorry to say she a crack head turning tricks, and he just one of many, Lord ham mercy!" Pausing she takes a breath and asks, "Little Hannah, what's going on in your life nowadays? I see some man got you on lock down cause he got two rangs on yo fanger."

"Yes Ma'am. I am married and we have a daughter."

"What you say! My how precious that is. Good for you Hannah. So what brings you back to Kristina then since now I know it ain't Leroy?

"Miss. Ann."

"Come again. Now I ain't never thought I would hear that. Sometimes I just knew they was gone find that woman dead in that house one day cause the evil in yo eyes had an appointment for her murder."

"Was I that bad Mrs. Frank?"

"Worse. You was most definitely worse. You ever wonder why those other lil kids didn't play with you? Baby they was scare you would choke em out if they beat you at games. Mean as a toothless vipor."

Hannah and Mrs. Frank laugh at that one."But I always liked you cause I know you was like that for a reason." Leaning forward as if no one else could hear the conversation she asks, "Why you looking for Ann."

"You wouldn't believe me if I told you."

"Try me. I got a black president, what you got?"

"God sent me."

"Umm. Well He is one to get His point across now ain't He?"

"You have no idea. I really need to speak with her."

"Baby I honestly don't know where she could be. Rumor has it she fell off the face of the earth. Truth is if she did I'll be the first to dance on her grave. Say she got religion for real the last time. I don't know but she think I didn't know her stanky butt was knocking boots with my ole man all that time. That thang was something else, her. You want to bet I had the last laugh cause he raised four kids but only one of them his and you could guess which one…yup, Leroy. Wasn't no love in that one that night. Just gin and vodka. See that's why you don't drink baby." Making a face she vigorously shakes her head and repeats her last statement, "That is the main reason you don't drink."

When the old deacon wonders in and sees Hannah sitting at the table with his wife Hannah was certain he was going to have a stroke. His face was contorted and his eyes bulged and he looked like he was staring death in the face.

"Look whose here Frank?" Little Hannah, all grown up and married now. Just as pretty as a picture. Got a lil girl too, ain't that something?"

Death struck he forces out, "Yeah, now that's something."

"She needs our help Frank. She's trying to find Ann. Do you know where she can find her?"

Stuttering and stammering he manages to say, "Now…now…now Odessa, I aint got nothing to do with that."

"Nothing to do with what, helping an old friend out? This child has traveled all the way from Texas to see her and I know you are not going to let her trip be in vain. Are you Frank?"

"Now I can't help it at all if that happens. Ain't none of my business."

"Now this baby got to obey God and ***** you gon help her. Where is Ann? Frank? Where is she or you gon be sleeping out there with the mutt you brought home yesterday. Talking bout none of yo business. It was yo business when you was creeping. Maybe I should talk to Little Hannah some more. I'm sure she could tell me a thing or two that might help me if I ever decided to…I don't know, go to court."

"See baby, that ain't even necessary. Nobody sayin nothing bout no court now. Miss. Hannah, I heard she over in Westmore."

The odd couple forgets all about their guest at that point.

"Westmore! Westmore! You mean Ann cracked up? Well fly me backwards and shoot me in the butt with a pellet gun. Who told you that?"

"Heard Odessa, that's what I say I heard."

"You know good and bleep, bleep, bleep well you know exactly where she is so don't play games with me Frank or I will bust you in the head with yo mama's iron skillet."

"Odessa…Odessa, why you got to be so violent, now that ain't Christian like."

"How would you know Frank, huh? How on earth would you know?" Looking over she sees Hannah and remembers they still have a guest. "Tell her the truth Frank or I swear on yo daddy's false teeth I'll be single by Christmas. Talk! You bald head scalawag!"

Clearing his throat Mr. Frank does precisely what he was told to do. "Well, round bout this time last year she started to look real bad. Losing weight and barely going out the house. Some of the church members got concerned and went round to check on her but couldn't get it. So one of the old mothers dialed 911 and that is when they found her laying up in the bed almost dead. They put her in the hospital, but she didn't get any better. Wouldn't eat, talk to nobody, just lay there and stare at the wall all day. Since she didn't have any kin folks to claim her or help her out the state sent her to Westmore and she been there ever since."

Feeling sick to her stomach Hannah asks, "Where may I find this Westmore?"

Mr. Frank is quick to answer now. "Next town over. Take the turnpike and get off on the second exit and make a left. You will see it bout five miles down the road. You can't miss it cause there is a big dog food plant right next to it."

Getting up to leave she hugs Mrs. Frank and thanks them both for their help and hospitality. The seven mile drive back to the hotel was like an eternity. Brice took one look at her and knew things were about to get interesting.

Chapter 25

After talking with her husband that night and then with her mother the next morning they prayed as a family. Brice decided that Hannah would not go alone although she tried to convince him otherwise. Johanna would stay back at the hotel with Joy who was starting to run a low grade fever. The Florida weather had been a drastic change for her little body. She was dealing with a whole new realm of allergens and she wasn't fairing too well.

When Brice and Hannah pull into the parking lot of the Westmore Mental Institution they remain in the car for a few minutes. She was gathering her courage and he was praying for his wife. The plan had been to find her birth mother and make peace, beyond that Hannah had no other plan. God had promised to be with her and that was what she was depending on. When Brice reaches for the door she stops him.

"Brice, I need to do this alone."

His reply was immediate, "Over my dead body."

"Please Brice, I will be fine. God told me it was going to be alright and I believe Him. I need to do this alone. Besides, I have my phone and if I am gone too long come looking for me, call the police or whatever you deem necessary."

"Hannah I am your husband and I am going to be by your side."

"Please Brice. Everything you've asked me I've done it or I've given it. You always say I am the best thing that has ever happened to you but the truth is you are the best gift I have ever been given. You and Joy are my life and I am so happy to be Mr. Chandler's Wife. This time I am asking you to trust me, please Brice. I must face her alone."

"You know I am struggling with this one Han. It is just not proper for me to sit here and do nothing while you are facing only God knows what in there. I promised to be there and I feel so useless. Plus I just want to be assured that you are safe because that is what a husband does for his wife. I can't see beyond those walls so how can I protect you Baby?"

"God has me. He has us and He always has, you taught me that Ant."

Groaning rather loudly he gives in. "You have thirty minutes and I am coming in after you."

When the doors closed behind Hannah panic seized her when she realized that there were no handles from the inside of the ward. She was trapped inside a mental institution. Even if it was for a visit, it could not end soon enough. The front desk was just a few feet from the locked double doors so she figured the sooner she completed her mission the better.

"Excuse me, I am here to see Miss. Antoinette Hardy please."

The nurses look at each other before one of them slowly get up from the lounge chair where they have both been watching a popular sitcom. "I'm sorry Ma'am but Miss. Hardy is not permitting to have visitors."

"Why would that be Ms….?"

"Davis. I'm Ms. Davis, head nurse to be exact. I don't make the rules Miss. I just enforce them."

"Well Ms. Davis I'd like to speak to someone that does so I will be able to see Miss. Hardy." By this time the other nurse is not so interested in watching her show. She joins Nurse Davis at the desk and adds, "She is only allowed to see family Miss, no one else."

Curt to say the least, Hannah replies, "And you are?"

"Mrs. Jackson" she responds through closed lips proceeded by hunched shoulders.

"Ms. Davis and Mrs. Jackson I am a relative and I would be overjoyed if you would be so kind and show me to the room of Antoinette Rachel Hardy."

"That's not going to happen lady. Miss Hardy doesn't have any relatives so you must be mistaken. Now if you would be so kind as to turn around and walk back through those doors we won't have to call security!"

"Security works for me because I will not be leaving until I have been allowed to see Miss. Hardy. So go ahead and make your call. I will wait."

The nurses stare at Hannah and she does not so much as flinch. Her heart told her something wasn't right. Why were they so adamant about her not seeing Miss. Ann? How could they be so sure she had no relatives? After a minute or two of silence wars Ms. Davis sucks her teeth and says, "ID please" and throws a clip board in front of Hannah demanding she sign in and gives her a badge to wear. "All personal items must remain at the front desk and you are not permitted to give patients outside food, weapons, drugs, cigarettes, or any such thing that may cause them to harm themselves or the staff."

Nurse Jackson tells her to, "Go straight through those double doors, make a right, then a quick left and follow the signs Miss."

When she says "Thank you" the nurse doesn't answer.

Hannah literally felt like someone had placed a bag over her head and was pulling it in a death grip. She saw people bound in strait jackets, some gagged and others in corners afraid to look you in the eye. There were rockers, tappers, head bangers, scab pickers, and then there were the cursers; all under one roof. When she finally found Miss. Ann's room she was relieved.

At first she only peered in the padded room with no windows. Just like in her dream there were several machines going. There is no movement. She watched the rise and fall of Miss. Ann's chest to know for certain that she had not expired. Entering the small room the smell of urine and feces hit her like black ice in winter storm. No warning just pending destruction. Walking over to the bed her heart was seized with compassion. No one should have to live that way, but even worse die in such an inhuman way.

"Miss. Ann…it's Hannah." Touching her arm she spoke a little louder. "It's Hannah Miss. Ann. I wanted to tell you I'm sorry for hating you so much and for not wanting to forgive you. Maybe you had your reasons for the way you treated me, I don't know, but I do understand now that it had to take a lot of courage to come to me like you did a couple of years ago. Pausing she tried to remember if she was remembering all of the speech she had been rehearsing since leaving the parking lot. She didn't know, but she felt like she had covered the basics.

"Well, I just needed you to know that it is alright now. I've started over and I want you to be able to do the same thing."

Standing there for a while she listens to the whistling and squishing of the machines. For some reason she thought something miraculous was going to take place when she uttered those words. Maybe some bright light from heaven or Jesus would suddenly enter the room. Perhaps some handwriting on the wall or something, anything; it had not. Miss. Ann was just as still as when she first entered the room. Looking at her so sick, so helpless, she was human to Hannah probably for the very first time. All humans felt pain, suffered lost, had disappointments, and made bad choices. She had not considered that before. She assumed all adults knew what to do, but after becoming an adult herself she found that was far from the truth.

Needing to make some connection with her before she left Hannah stepped closer to the bed and puts her head on Miss. Ann's head and says, "Oh Mom, how I wish things could have been much different. I needed you so badly. I am really sorry for everything. Your everything and my everything." Kissing her on the head she bolted from the room.

Running she tried to remember her way back to the front desk but gets lost within the institution. Overwhelmed she resisted the urge to scream. She did not want to be mistaken for one of the inpatients. She waited to see if some staff member would happen by so she could get some directions, but after an hour passes and all she heard were the patients on the ward talking to themselves or banging on the padded walls she knew she was in a horrid predicament.

Where was Brice? Her phone did not have any reception and all she saw ahead of her was an endless white hall. Surrounded by chaos and mentally challenged people she wondered if she was losing her mind. Walking briskly she turns abruptly feeling someone's touch, but no one was there. She fights the fear that attempted to grip her soul. It becomes unclear about the voices she hears. Were they in her head or was it the patients in the distance? Westmore was a completely and utterly hopeless place and she could see it, smell it, and feel it. Who could ever survive in a place like this she asked herself over and over. On the brink of mental exhaustion she cries out, "God help me out of here and I promise I will get her out of this place."

The words were barely out of her mouth and a man appears preparing to clean the floors of the institution and notices her.

"Miss., may I help you with something?"

"Yes, I do believe I'm lost. How do I find the front desk?"

"Which front desk is that Miss.?"

"9 C."

"You really are lost. This is 9A."

"Let me radio security and we'll get you there. I'm not allowed to let anyone in or out you see."

"Understood." Hannah tries to calm herself while she waits for her rescue. By the time someone arrived to escort her to the front desk it was another twenty minutes. How could the care be so awful and the concern so little for the patients?

When Hannah at last returns to the front desk Brice is there with four police officers and several other important looking people. What she doesn't know is that she has been missing for two and a half hours and for the last hour they have been policing the area searching for one Mrs. Hannah Chandler.

"Oh Baby, I was so worried about you. You didn't answer your phone and no one seemed to know anything. According to the facility no such person had ever entered the building."

"What, they made me leave everything at the desk, and my cell phone would not pick up reception inside this building. Then I became lost and there was no one to help me. Brice I should have listened to you. This place is appalling. Just horrific."

Throwing herself into his arms she says, "She can't stay here Brice. I don't care what has happened, I can't leave her here. I just won't."

"I'm just glad you're fine Baby. You tell me what we need to do and it is done."

Hannah walks to one of the police officers and tells him where she left her purse. When he escorts her to the station of Nurse Davis and Jackson they suddenly have amnesia.

"Good Evening Miss. it's a good day at Westmore. How may I serve you?"

Not believing her ears Hannah gives Ms. Davis the I can't believe it look, but nurse, I have two people living inside me continued with her little game.

"I left my purse with you and Nurse Jackson and I would like to have it back please."

"Certainly Ma'am" Ms. Davis replies, I hope your visit with Miss. Hardy was a pleasant one."

Hannah ignored them both after taking her purse and walks away with her husband. Thanking the police officer she asks, "Officer how would I get someone to inspect this place because I know it is not up to standard. My mother's room is awful and I know she is not being cared for humanly. She has sores and the food she is being feed I am sure is rotten."

"Miss. we are already one step ahead of you. When your husband insisted we find his wife or he was calling the news stations, the Mayor and the President if need be, we found some god awful things ourselves in the search. We have already called in a few people. I have a feeling this place is not going to be open much longer."

"Oh thank God for that. I must get my mother out of here before they kill her."

"I do not blame you for that Miss. Make sure you speak to those people right over there and file a report. Keep a copy for yourself you hear." He walks a few feet, then turns and says, "If you ever need anything give me a holler" and gives Hannah a card and his badge number.

Brice thanks him for his help and he waves good-bye. Once Hannah speaks to the officials and does the proper paper work they head back to the hotel exhausted. It was not until the next morning that Hannah and Brice actually talk about the visit and what happened at the institution.

"Brice I promised God I would get her out of there."

"Han I am with you one thousand percent. That place should not take care of dead people, let alone living ones."

They'd later learned that no one came to see the patients at Westmore. The patients there had no one left to care or no one knew where they were. No one checked to see how they were being treated, no one checked to see if they were receiving proper treatment, no one saw that they bathed or ate. Hannah had seen carts of food trays sitting at the entrance of the wards until someone from the cafeteria came and rolled them out again. They had never been given to the starving patients that needed them.

They all knew what must happen but had no idea how it was going to come to fruition. Joy still wasn't feeling well and they had three days to figure out what to do about Miss. Ann. Johanna's answer of course was prayer. That was always her answer to everything. If you asked her why she just said, "Prayer is always a good start in the right direction; can't go wrong with that." So they prayed all Wednesday morning and took care of little Joy. By that evening there still was not an answer until Brice suddenly flashes his goofy smile and announces he has a plan.

"Let's call Officer Jones. He said he would help us if we needed it and we need it."

"What can he do Brice?"

"He can help you find a judge to get an emergency court order and get temporary guardianship. He has to know someone."

"Just in case this miracle takes place, then what?"

We get her out of there, into a place that is going to help her and then we go from there Han. Let's get her well first. If that means we have her transferred to San Antonio then that is what we will do."

Johanna begins to laugh. "I believe my son is on to something there Baby Girl."

"Give me the phone please." Hannah was starting to believe.

That was the start of many small miracles that lead to numerous other miracles. Officer Aiden Jones did know someone who knew someone that knew someone that played golf with a judge. Hannah was going to have her day in court.

Chapter 26

Deciding against the elevator, Hannah nervously throws open the door to the stairs and sprints the two flights of stairs in her four inch heels to the third floor. The dress she wore resembled something clergy would wear to the bedside of an ailing parishioner. Grey, dismal, buttoned to the neckline and extending far below the knees, it told no story of who was wearing such a garment. Trepidations stealing the air from her body she franticly searches each door of the large federal building. Her watch ticks like a bomb as to the nearing time of her appointment. She had exactly sixty seconds before the doors would be secured and there would be nothing left for her to do; the fight would end and possibly a life. Her heart stands before her God as she inwardly reminds Him that all of this was His idea and she was only attempting to honor His wishes. She stops to catch her breath in a half attempt to slow the rapid heart rate she was experiencing. Once again she reminds God that it is all in His hands. "If this is what you truly want, you will have to make the way, I'm willing."

When a police officer appeared before her she marveled that she never heard him approaching. "Miss, may I assist you?" The Caucasian giant of a man asks in a mousey voice.

"I sure hope so. If you would please point me in the direction of the probate court sir I would be most appreciative."

With a flash of the most beautiful teeth he responds, "Just turn around. The sign is being replaced, but I assure you when you walk in you will find precisely what you need."

Literally running through the door Hannah finds her place seconds before the bailiff announces, "All rise, The honorable judge William Sache preceding…" In sitting down the mad rush of Monday morning traffic, the all-nighter with a feverish two year old, and the absence of legal support all sat with her. Glad her case was not first she concentrates on breathing and nothing else. No rehearsed words, no speeches, the truth was all she was working with.

It wasn't long before her case was before the judge. Hannah expected a battle, but there wasn't one. She presented documentation that she had been a ward of Miss. Ann. She stated that now she wanted to in turn care for her now that she was in need. She presented financial documentation that she was financially sound, proof of residence that she was stable, and a background check that hopefully proved she was good citizen. After presenting those documents she presented the pictures that she'd taken from her cell phone which were now enlarged. She had statements from the state inspection that had taken place that night she visited Miss. Ann and a copy of the police report and their findings. The court already had copies of Miss. Ann's medical records.

The judge was slow in viewing the documents. Deliberately looking through each piece of paper there was no urgency for him. "Young lady do you realize that this is a great responsibility?"

"Yes Your Honor, I have weighed the matter and it is not only something I must do, but something I want to do."

"Why do you want to take on such a huge responsibility Mrs. Chandler?"

"She took care of me when I had no one else Sir. I do not feel obligated as in tasked, but I do feel it is a part of me honoring her according to what the Bible says about the treatment of your parents. Not doing anything at all would hurt me more than helping her ever could."

"What kind of support system do you have Mrs. Chandler?"

"I have a loving husband who is behind me one hundred percent…"

"Where is this husband?" he interrupts.

"He is back at the hotel Your Honor, caring for our daughter who is running a fever."

"I see…go on. What other support do you have Mrs. Chandler?"

"I have the support of my god-mother who is also with us on this trip, a few close friends and a great church family. My brother also provides a great deal of support and strength to me, plus the strength that I receive from my faith in God sir."

"Your brother Mrs. Chandler, where is he?"

"My half-brother sir, and he resides in Richmond, Virginia but we have a very close relationship."

"How would you like the court to act on your behalf Mrs. Chandler?"

"Your Honor my mother will die, I am certain of it, if she is not immediately removed from the Westmore Institute. She is a beautiful woman, only fifty years old. Here is a picture of her at age forty-five. Now look at the picture taken just three days ago Your Honor." Giving the photos to the bailiff she continues to speak. "Please allow her to be placed in a hospital so she may receive complete physical examinations so then she will be properly placed to receive adequate treatment. I want to bring her home with me to San Antonio so that I may provide care for her until she is well again. Here is a list of facilities that are able to provide care for her in my area until that time."

"You have certainly done your homework Mrs. Chandler." Nodding she waits for his decision.

"In the case of ward Antoinette Rachel Hardy, full guardianship has been awarded to her daughter, Hannah Renee Corel-Waiters Chandler. Having not been found of a sound mind and is mentally and physically incapacitated, Mrs. Chandler assumes full responsibility and care of Miss. Hardy and her estate and will report to the courts semiannually the where bouts of Miss. Hardy. The court also grants the request of Conservatorship to Mrs. Chandler and is aware that financial reports must be filed with the court on an annual basis. A court appointed social worker will assigned to this case for the next year. After that we will bring this matter before the court again to see what is best for Miss. Hardy."

Life collides with her head and she is assured she is about to have a panic attack, but remembered to think, "I'm strong and I can do this", and exhales.

When the judge says, "Congratulations Mrs. Chandler." She really did not believe it was time for a congratulatory moment, but she says a gracious, "Thank you" for kindness sake.

Surreal astonishment escorted her from the courtroom and her mind goes back to the events of the last several months. What a ride of highs and lows it had been. If anyone had told her about this day she surely would have thought them to be insane.

Before getting on the road Saturday Hannah visits Miss. Ann once more. She is a different person this time. Having been moved to the best hospital in the region, the threatening of a lawsuit being a motivator, she was getting state of the art care.

When Hannah walks in her birth mother's eyes swell with tears. "I thought I dreamed it, but you really are here."

"Yes Ma'am and you look so much better. I have to go but I promise I will be back to get you. The nurses and the doctors have all of my contact information and will give me a daily report."

"Thank you Hannah. Thank you so much." She looks down suddenly as in shame. When she starts ringing her hands Hannah places her hands over them to still them and tells her, "It's the past."

"Please forgive me. I am so sorry for the way I treated you. He rejected me, so I rejected you. I wanted someone to love me so badly and I put all my faith and hope in him. When I told him about my pregnancy he made it clear I had only been a fling and he had no intention of staying around for me or for my baby. I was too blind to see God had given me someone to love and that you were my miracle. All I saw was how much you looked like him and I transferred my rejection, shame, and hatred of him to you. That was wrong."

"Oh Miss. Ann…that is the past and I don't want either of us to live there anymore?"

Shaking her head she looks at Hannah like it is the last time she will ever see her.

"You're going to be just fine. I know you still have a long road to recovery but I will be there with you if that is alright."

"That is great Hannah."

"How does San Antonio sound?"

She weeps then and nothing can stop the tears. When Hannah waves to her with the promise of calling the next day she is still weeping.

Chapter 27

Exhausted physically and mentally Hannah sleeps much of the ride back to San Antonio. They don't have a lot of time so they push it and do the entire trip in a day. Partly because she wants to get her own baby to the doctor. She hated when her poor little baby wasn't feeling well. All she wanted to do was hold her daughter and make her better. Going home she places Johanna up front and she sits with her in the back holding her hand and singing when she had those moments that she was high spirited. They had taken her to an urgent care facility in the area just to satisfy the three of them, but they diagnosed her with a cold, and sent them on their way. Her mother was certain they were wrong and already had an appointment with her pediatrician that Sunday afternoon in his weekend clinic.

Her other reason for wanting to get back was her husband. He needed some rest before having to return to work Monday morning. He had been such a rock during everything they encountered during the past several days. God she loved him more each day. He refused to allow her or her mother to drive although they were quite capable. She was concerned that he still did not want to talk about the drama on Thanksgiving Day, but she prayed about it all the time.

Several times during the course of the trip home their eyes meet in the rearview mirror sending messages back and forth without saying a word. They drew on each other's strength and she understood more and more what it meant to become one in a marriage. She would probably never comprehend why he cheated, but she gave up the torturer of trying to figure it out. They would move past it and build a life together. The only thing her heart longed for was to give him a son. Maybe when the time was right and their lives were finally settled they would talk about adoption, if he agreed.

When they hit the San Antonio city limits they all breathe a sigh of relief. Joy who should have been asleep at ten o'clock at night yelled out, "Woo Hoo!" Recognizing the sports arena and the bridge they crossed to get home. After dropping her mother off they take a detour by the pharmacy and pick up some items for Joy. When they pull into their garage Hannah doesn't know who is most excited of her family members, but guessed it was probably Brice. Leading your family could not be the easiest job in the world.

The next hour Hannah dedicated to unpacking, giving Joy her medicines, bath, bedtime story, and finally to taking a long hot shower. Brice takes the car through the car wash, gases up for the week, and then irons his cloths for work on Monday. He knows she will do it the next day but Hannah honestly thinks it is his way of winding down. When Hannah comes out of her hygiene hibernation she is ready to answer some of those love looks her husband was sending to her on the trip back. She wanted to tell him and show him how much he was appreciated for doing all the things he did for his family. Her plans come to a screeching halt when she enters their bedroom and finds her husband lying across the bed in his boxers fast asleep. She turns out the lights and follow suit.

Hannah sleeps hard, so hard her cell phone rings three times before she hears it and then she can't find it. Rolling over to greet her husband she discovers he was not next to her. The clock on the wall said ten a.m. and she was stunned. Leaping from the bed she first goes to Joy's room. She'd intended to set an alarm to check her temperature during the night and give her more medicine but forgot. Joy was not in her bed. Turning she heads to the living room and find the two cuddled up in a blanket watching cartoons.

"Look Joy, it's sleeping beauty" her husband teases when he sees her.

"No daddy, I sleeping beauty, that's Mommy!"

"May I join the party" she asks kissing them both good morning.

"Mommy sit by me." Joy gets excited and starts a fit of coughing which leads to vomiting, a shower, and a lot of extra hugs and kisses from them both. The doctor's appointment confirms Hannah's suspicions. Joy has an upper respiratory infection and it takes a few days and two different types of antibiotics before she feels better. For this reason Hannah does not venture far from their home. She takes care of her family and nothing else. This was her life for the next several weeks, rebuilding and healing her family. Johanna was included in their healing process.

As promised, she checks on Miss. Ann daily and even briefly speaks to her between test and mandatory evaluations. Johanna visits often and is always doing little things, which are great things for them, which included spending quality time with her children. The shocker, she was actually dating after over twenty years of being single and serving the church. Hannah had to admit her new beau was a nice man and no one deserved nice like Johanna did so she accepted their relationship.

Jane visits more as well. One day she drops a bomb shell on her. "How would you feel if I dated Ian?"

"Excuse me! Stop the elevator because I have got to be on the wrong floor."

"You don't have to be like that Han. He's a good guy and well I kind of like him and I think he may just like me too. I just want to know how you feel about it before I do anything that's all."

"So you are saying if I say not no but never would I want that to ever happen in this life or in any other, you would be fine with that?"

"Dang Han you don't have to be so cruel. I know I have had a man or two, but I think anyone can change with God's help. You have proven that to me more than anyone I know Han. Plus, I always feel so much better when I talk to him. It is like I can see my life becoming good and whole."

"Maybe it is God you long for and not Ian. You just feel it more when you are around him because he has such a close relationship with God."

"You may be right."

"Promise me you will take the next ninety days and go on a journey with God. No interference of the testosterone nature. After that, then see how you feel. If it is meant to be, by then you will know it."

"Child since when did you get a degree in catch a manology!"

"Life honey, plus I have been reading Brice's counseling material when he is not around."

Hannah's relationships are growing stronger and better and she is thankful each day. She and Ian or Tobias was always on the phone or texting, and Michael thinks he is her daddy. Miss. Ann was one step closer to moving to San Antonio. Johanna has taken it upon herself to be a friend to her and the two talked often. Although Miss. Ann was on a ton of medications, everything from antidepressants to high blood pressure medication, she was still much better off than what she had ever been because her guilt was no longer a factor. She saw a physiatrist twice weekly and was making progress according to her doctor.

The other Chandlers were on mute again, but other than that life was good, really good. She was loving on her husband and sexing him up each opportunity she was given. He was doing drive bys for lunch for quickies. They talked as well as played. Most of all their family has begun to attend church regularly again. For the first time in her life she was not worrying about anything. Not, Brice cheating again, losing God, Miss. Ann, or Joy. She took each day as it came and enjoyed it whole heartedly.

Life was the perfect she'd secretly prayed it would be. Until one day a sheriff with a subpoena made an appearance at her doorstep on a windy Tuesday morning. She assumed it was something from the courts about Miss. Ann, but from the corner of her eye she saw the state of Washington. Her heart literally dropped to the floor. Opening the letter with shaking hands she learned that Connor was suing her for custody of their daughter. On grounds that she was an unfit mother, unstable, and his daughter was not safe being in the constant environment of the mentally ill.

When Brice answered his phone she was screaming and he was unable to comprehend anything she said. Attempting to calm her he asked questions and when he got to Joy she screamed even louder. He left his job then. His heart and his head told him there would not be a quick fix for their current crisis.

When he arrived home nothing could have prepared him for the condition of his wife. Slumped over in a corner, hair matted to her face from the salty tears that had soaked her blouse and made a puddle on the floor. She screamed constantly to the air, "Why, why God why! I did everything you asked me to do. Why God! She's all I have. You already have my other babies, why does this have to happen? Have I behaved that badly? He doesn't love her. He has never even seen her. Why why why?" she moaned over and over again.

Brice still unsure of what had taken place picks her up and takes her to their bedroom. He washes her face and cleans her nose and brushes her hair back and puts a clip on it. She was still sobbing profusely while rocking back and forth in the bed when he went back to their living room and retrieved the papers that fell from her hands when he picked her up. He prayed, knowing it was bad news. Before reading the papers he texted Johanna and asked her if she would come over very soon. She knew something was very wrong as well. Next he asked Jane to allow Joy and RJ's play date to be extended and he would explain later. Then he read the official court documents.

Brice, the husband, the father, the man, did not cry. He became angry when he found out what Connor was up to and vowed he would never have his daughter. When Johanna arrived she also reads the documents and makes some phone calls. She felt her daughter was going to need a good attorney and some prayer warriors on her side. By the end of the night she had both. That day her mother spends the night with them and little Joy sleeps in her parent's bed. Hannah doesn't eat or drink that day or for the next several days.

For the following days war went on in the Chandler's home. Numerous phone calls end bitterly when she tried to reason with Connor.

"You have never seen her Connor."

"You never gave me that chance Renee! Then you give her some other man's name. How dare you!" Pure venom spewed from his mouth.

"She is the only one that will be hurt in this Connor. Brice is the only father she knows. Not once since I called you have you ever tried to contact me about seeing her."

"It took you how long to tell me about her? You have nothing to say to me Renee."

"Your father hates people of color. How do you think he is going to feel about her? How do you think he is going to treat her? What about your new wife? Will she accept my baby and love her like I do?"

"All of that is none of your concern. I told you once not to cross me, now I am going to make a believer out of you. See you in court!"

Resolving to take the advice of her attorneys she deems it necessary to know her enemy. He had been monitoring everything about her life for the past several months. He was aware of her and Brice's separation, her losing her job, the hospital stay, Miss. Ann, and what she ate for breakfast each day. He knew about Joy's allergies and each hospital visit. He had done his home work so now it was time for her to do her own.

Mysteriously, Connor had taken a wife after finding out about Joy. Penelope Rinehart, the only daughter of a multimillionaire. She had come from money, been sent to the finest schools, studied abroad and was well known in the Washington area. Her father was the opposite. Growing up in the Midwest, the son of a farmer, he had gotten his break by inventing a piece of farm equipment that revolutionized the farming industry. Later at the bidding of a friend he invested in some internet stock and their lives were set forever. When his wife contracted a debilitating illness they relocated to Washington so she would have the best medical treatment. Penelope was twelve years old at the time.

Other than a few minor traffic violations Connor appeared to be squeaky clean. That worried Hannah. She thought of the many things he could and would bring to the courtroom to vengefully take her daughter away from her. All the intimate secrets they'd shared during love making. He knew too much about her and she knew too little about him.

Hannah felt defeated when their court day finally arrived. Connor plays the role of a perfect father that only longed for a relationship with the daughter he never had knowledge existed. He makes out as the saint and Hannah is the villain. The judge eats everything he feeds him. Anytime she attempted to add something the judge dismissed her.

When it was all said and done Connor is awarded joint custody and the terms of the custody demanded that Joy slowly transitions to having a life with her birth father. Until she enters school Joy must spend six months with her father in Washington and six months in Texas with her mother. Holidays would be alternated between the parents and Connor was free to take her out of the country without permission from her mother. The courts ordered that an official name change be completed to make Joy's last name Lee not Chandler.

All are devastated. Even Johanna's faith is shaken. She had been confident that Sister Lucy had been speaking of this situation when she suddenly turned to her daughter and said, "You win, remember that" on Thanksgiving Day, but Hannah had not won. Connor did and as a result none of their lives would ever be the same. There would be a transition period for Joy to spend time with her birth father and then she was to fly out to Washington for one week during spring break.

The only reason Hannah doesn't collapse in the midst of it all was because her husband was holding onto one side of her and her mother held onto the other side. No one could do anything about her shattered heart.